W9-DBC-431

LOIS FAYE DYER

THE COWBOY TAKES A WIFE

SPECIAL ▼ EDITION®

Published by Silhouette Books
America's Publisher of Contemporary Romance

For RoseMarie Lunny-Harris and Barbara South,
who critiqued, encouraged, prodded and threatened
until I *finally* became published.
Whatever would I do without friends like you?

 SILHOUETTE BOOKS

ISBN 0-373-24198-4

THE COWBOY TAKES A WIFE

Copyright © 1998 by Lois Faye Dyer

Books by Lois Faye Dyer

Silhouette Special Edition

Lonesome Cowboy #1038
He's Got His Daddy's Eyes #1129
The Cowboy Takes a Wife #1198

LOIS FAYE DYER

Winner of the 1989-1990 *Romantic Times* Reviewer's Choice Award for Best New Series Author, Lois Faye Dyer lives on Washington State's beautiful Puget Sound with her husband and their yellow Lab, Maggie Mae. She ended a career as a paralegal and superior court clerk to fulfill a life-long dream to write. When she's not involved in writing, she enjoys long walks on the beach with her husband, watching musical and Western movies from the 1940s and 1950s and, most of all, indulging her passionate addiction to reading. This is her tenth published novel.

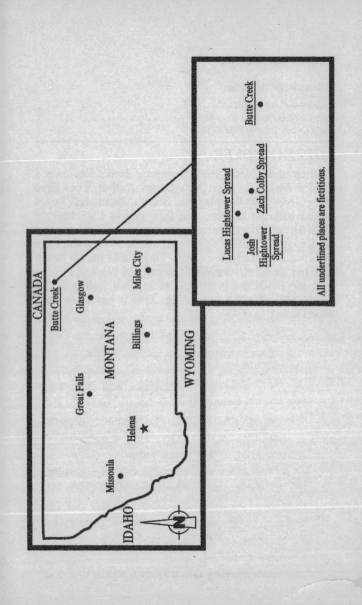

CANADA

Butte Creek

Glasgow

Great Falls

MONTANA

Missoula

Helena

Billings

Miles City

WYOMING

IDAHO

N

Butte Creek

Lucas Hightower Spread

Zach Colby Spread

Josh
Hightower
Spread

All underlined places are fictitious.

Chapter One

A gray, early November sky hovered low over the Montana prairie. The cold wind whipped at the dried yellow grass and carried a brief smattering of icy snow pellets.

Zach Colby eyed the leaden skies and flicked on the windshield wipers to remove flakes that were half ice, half snow. Outside, the temperature dropped steadily, but inside the cab of the big four-wheel-drive pickup he was warm and comfortable.

Dwight Yoakam's voice poured out of the stereo speakers, the lyrics to "A Thousand Miles From Nowhere" filling the interior. Zach reached out and pushed the eject button; the cassette tape popped out, and the radio—tuned to the local Scobey, Montana, station—came to life.

"...the front moving down from Canada is a cold

one, folks. Better get out your thermal underwear and parkas—this storm is showing all the signs of giving our corner of northeast Montana the first really serious snow of the winter. And now a word from our sponsor—''

Zach switched off the radio and scowled out the windshield at the ribbon of two-lane blacktop stretching ahead of him. He was twenty miles north of Wolf Point; he had another thirty miles to drive before he reached Butte Creek, and thirty miles beyond that to his ranch. He hoped the snow didn't get worse before then, but he had little faith that the falling flakes wouldn't thicken. Impatient though he was to reach home and the innumerable chores awaiting him, he forced himself to keep the throttle at a steady, even speed.

The odometer had ticked off three miles when he crested a rise and instantly eased the pressure on the gas pedal. A small blue car was pulled onto the graveled shoulder of the road, the left rear fender barely off the blacktop. The right rear tire was flat, and a figure bundled in a bulky winter coat and ski cap was bent over the open trunk.

"Oh, hell," he muttered. He tapped the brakes gently and the big truck eased to a full stop a short distance past the car. The engine rumbled when he shifted into reverse and backed up the highway to pull in behind the disabled vehicle. Switching on the flashing emergency lights, he left the engine running and thrust open the door to step outside. The wind caught at his unbuttoned coat, cold air knifing through the plaid wool shirt and thermal undershirt he wore beneath the heavy sheepskin-lined jacket.

CeCe Hawkins had never been so glad to see another human being in her life. Changing a flat tire in a maintenance class at home in Seattle was one thing, actually having to accomplish the task on a deserted snowy highway was something else entirely.

The driver stepped out of the truck and walked toward her through the fall of steadily increasing snowflakes, buttoning his coat as he approached. He was tall, his shoulders broad under a thigh-length, rough suede jacket. Denim jeans covered his long legs and his black cowboy boots crunched over the deepening snow.

"Hello," she called as he neared. "Am I glad to see you!"

The husky feminine contralto jolted Zach. Throaty and seductive, it was a voice to keep a man hot, bothered and awake nights. It shook his usual cool composure and he flicked a swift, assessing glance over her. Wisps of dark brown hair escaped from beneath a forest green ski hat and brushed the smooth skin of cheeks stung pink by the cold wind. Thick black lashes framed dark gray eyes and the soft curve of her mouth was lush, the bottom lip fuller than the top. A swift image of gently biting that soft fullness before soothing the sting with his tongue sent a surge of purely sexual adrenaline through his veins.

Shocked by the unexpected force of his reaction, he dragged his gaze away from her and focused it on the car. The back seat was piled high with boxes and bags. "Are you out here alone?"

"I'm afraid so." CeCe clutched the tire iron she'd been holding a little tighter. Up close, the big man was intimidating. Shielded from the falling snow by the brim of his black Stetson, his handsome face was all hard angles with sharply defined cheekbones and a stubborn jaw. His tanned skin was marred by the white slash of a scar that grooved his left cheek from just in front of his ear to an inch before the corner of his mouth.

Beneath tawny eyebrows, his ice blue eyes were winter-cold as they quickly assessed her. Something hot and untamed flared briefly in his gaze, too, but it fled so quickly that CeCe decided she'd imagined his reaction. Stunned by her quickened heartbeat and the leap of heat in her veins, she looked away when he did to focus on the flat tire. "I must have picked up a nail or run over something sharp," she told him. "The tires are only a week old. I had them put on when I had the car serviced just before I left Seattle."

"Seattle?" Zach reached into the open trunk, glancing sideways at her while prying the spare tire free from among more tightly packed suitcases and boxes. A dark green jacket fell to mid-thigh, and the coat's tan corduroy collar was turned up to shield her throat, her chin tucked into its protection. Once again, he had to pull his gaze away from her and force himself to ignore his body's demand for attention while he tried to remember what he'd started to ask her. "You're not used to driving in snow, are you?"

"No," CeCe admitted. Unbidden, a smile curved her mouth. "In fact, when it snowed in Seattle, I left my car home and took the bus."

Zach shot her a quick, disbelieving glance before he lowered the spare tire to the ground, leaned it against the car's bumper and deftly took the tire iron from her gloved hands.

"Go get in my truck," he ordered. "No sense in both of us standing out here in the cold."

"Oh, but I..." CeCe started to protest, but the impatience written on his hard face made her reconsider. "All right," she conceded. "I guess you don't need my help."

She turned away and took two steps toward the big pickup before she slipped on a patch of ice. Her feet flew out from under her and she shrieked.

The cowboy caught her before she hit the ground, easily swinging her up in his arms. Startled, her heart pounding, CeCe clutched a handful of his coat collar and stared up into his face.

Zach's nostrils flared. She smelled like spicy flowers underlaid with the scent of warm woman. Despite the bulk of her coat, she was small and fragile and an unfamiliar surge of possessiveness hit him. His grip tightened and he shifted her closer, his head dipping a fraction toward hers before her eyes widened in wary surprise, halting his instinctive movement as surely as if she'd screamed "No."

"Thank you." CeCe's voice trembled. How much of the quiver in her words was caused by her near fall and how much by the overwhelming nearness of the big man—she couldn't have said.

Bare inches separated their faces and he was even more lethally attractive.

Hot awareness replaced the remoteness in his eyes

and his gaze fastened with searing intensity on hers. If it wasn't so patently impossible, she would have sworn that he'd been about to kiss her. If it wasn't equally impossible, she'd swear that she was gravely disappointed that he hadn't.

CeCe restrained a swift, unbidden urge to trace the sensual curve of his mouth with a curious forefinger. She searched for speech to break the small, intense silence and uttered the first words that came to mind. "If I'd fallen, I might have hurt the baby."

Zach went completely still.

"Baby?"

CeCe let go of his jacket and shifted one hand to her midsection. "Yes—baby. I'm pregnant."

Disappointment slammed into him. *She belongs to someone.* Zach drew a deep breath and scowled at her, welcoming the rising anger that obscured the unreasonable sense of betrayal he felt. "You're pregnant," he repeated flatly, "and you're driving on roads you don't know in the middle of a snowstorm? Why the hell did your husband let you do something so idiotic?"

CeCe stiffened and frowned back at him. "*If* I had a husband, which I don't, he wouldn't *let* me do anything. I'm a grown woman. I make my own decisions."

"Hah," Zach growled in disgust. The brief tide of relief that she had no husband quickly retreated under the undeniable fact that she was pregnant. Just because she didn't have a husband didn't necessarily mean that there wasn't a man somewhere that claimed her as his own. "Anyone foolish enough to travel in this weather when they're not used to driving on snow-covered roads needs a keeper."

Still carrying her, he stalked to the passenger side of his truck. "Open the door."

Fuming, CeCe complied, and he swung her up onto the wide seat.

"Stay there till I get your tire changed," he ordered abruptly. Before she could respond, he slammed the door shut and stalked back to the little car.

The interior of the truck cab was toasty, the heater fan blowing a welcome blast of warm air against her cold toes. CeCe tugged off her wet gloves with jerky, impatient movements, and watched her rescuer change her tire with swift, economical ease.

"He thinks I need a keeper," she muttered. "What century is that man living in? I'll bet he doesn't even know that women have the right to vote."

She'd grown up in the cosmopolitan city of Seattle, had been engaged to her charming but unreliable college sweetheart before she was twenty-five, and had worked her way up the corporate ladder of a well-known department store chain to a respectable managerial level. At thirty-one, CeCe was accustomed to being independent. Even her loving parents had long ago recognized their second daughter's maturity. The man changing her tire had scooped her up in his arms as if she weighed no more than a baby and then proceeded to lecture her as if she were a child.

CeCe was not happy with him.

"On the other hand, he was nice enough to stop and help me," she reminded herself grudgingly, watching him pack the tire iron and car jack back into the trunk and close the lid.

Snow dusted his wide shoulders and the brim of his hat as he easily picked up the damaged tire and walked toward her. He disappeared toward the back of the truck, the cab rocking gently when he tossed the tire into the pickup bed. A moment later, the driver's door opened and a cold gust of air entered the cab. He slid beneath the wheel and slammed the door closed before glancing at her.

"The tread on your spare tire isn't the best. How far do you have to go?"

"To Butte Creek," she replied. "I think it might be another fifteen to twenty miles."

"Closer to thirty," he said, "but you should make it that far without trouble. I'll follow you there and drop your flat tire off at Jake's Garage to be repaired."

"Actually, my destination is a bit beyond Butte Creek."

"Yeah?" Zach wondered which of his neighbors she was visiting. "Where?"

"The Hall ranch. I understand it's another twenty to thirty miles west of town. Do you know it?"

Zach's fingers tightened over the steering wheel, his gaze narrowing as he stared at the brunette occupying the passenger seat of his truck. "I know it," he confirmed, his voice carefully noncommittal. "In fact, my place shares a fence line with it, but there's nobody there. The owner's been gone for nearly a year."

If he hadn't been watching her carefully, he might

have missed the brief flicker of sadness that moved swiftly across her expressive features.

"I know," she replied. "I recently inherited the property."

Zach didn't believe her.

The Hall ranch had been operated by Aaron Hall before he left town almost a year before, but he couldn't have willed the ranch to this woman. Aaron had the use of the land for his lifetime, but he didn't own it. And he could neither sell nor mortgage the valuable acres. His father, Kenneth Hall, had willed one-half of the estate to Aaron's children, the other half to Zach upon Aaron's death. If Aaron died without children, the entire estate went to Zach. The only thing Kenneth Hall had ever done to publicly recognize that Zach was his son was to name him as his beneficiary.

Butte Creek was a small, close-knit community. Zach knew that Aaron had been buried with minimal ceremony three weeks ago in the cemetery on the outskirts of town. Still, he'd put off visiting the attorney who handled the estate. He was reluctant to deal with the bad memories stirred up by Aaron's death and hadn't felt any urgency to claim his inheritance, knowing that the land itself would wait for his attention.

Sincere though she appeared, the woman had to be lying.

His gaze flicked to the woman's midsection, but her shape was indistinguishable beneath the bulky coat.

Unless she's Aaron's widow and the child she's

carrying is Aaron's. The thought hit Zach with stunning force.

The possibility that this woman, with her clear gray eyes and slender body, had belonged to his hated half brother elicited an immediate, violent rejection. Zach struggled to keep his face from reflecting the turmoil churning in his gut as he fished for the truth. "I thought the Hall place was still owned by Aaron Hall when he died. I'm surprised he sold out."

"Oh, he didn't," CeCe answered. "When Aaron passed away in October, he left the ranch to me and our daughter...or son." Her left hand, minus her discarded glove, spread in an unconsciously protective gesture over the dark green wool covering her midsection.

The movement caught Zach's gaze and his eyes narrowed over her slim, bare fingers. *Must have been some marriage,* he thought savagely. *She's already gotten rid of her wedding ring and he's only been gone a month.*

"I see," Zach said briefly, his voice devoid of emotion.

"If you share a fence line with the Hall ranch, then you must have known Aaron."

"I knew him."

Startled, CeCe glanced quickly at the rancher. His response to her innocent question carried an underlying tension that bordered on hostility. His expression was unreadable, however, and she decided she'd imagined his negative reaction.

"I'm Cecelia Hawkins," CeCe said belatedly,

holding out her hand. "If you share a fence line with the Hall ranch, then we must be neighbors."

"Zach Colby," he said brusquely. "I'm your closest neighbor." He didn't want to touch her, but his hard hand closed over her outstretched one, palm to palm, in a brief clasp before he gestured abruptly out the windshield at her car. "This weather isn't improving—in fact, it's getting worse. I'll follow you to the Hall place. Just stay on this highway until the second stoplight in Butte Creek, then turn left and keep driving west. I'll honk when we reach the turn-off."

"All right." CeCe fumbled with the door handle.

"Stay put," Zach ordered. "There's no sense in chancing another fall."

He shoved open his door and within minutes scooped CeCe from the passenger seat, strode across the snowy gravel and deposited her in the driver's seat of her own car.

"Just drive carefully—and slowly," he instructed her, his big frame blocking the wind from entering the wedge caused by the open door. "I'll be right behind you."

Before CeCe could respond, he closed the door.

"Thank you," she muttered to herself, her breath puffing clouds into the cold interior as she yanked her seat belt across her midriff and snapped it into the latch.

The engine stuttered, coughed and finally turned over with chilly reluctance.

"I don't blame you," CeCe commiserated, patting

the dashboard consolingly. "I don't like this cold weather either."

A throaty, growling complaint rumbled from a large cat carrier tucked among the boxes in the back seat.

"I hear you, Angus." She reached between the bucket seats and slipped her fingertips through the wire mesh in the big carrier's door to stroke the thick fur of the tomcat inside.

"I'll feed you as soon as we get there, okay?"

Angus purred his agreement and pushed against her fingers.

She waited several minutes, giving the cold engine time to warm up, before she put on her blinker, glanced at her side mirror and pulled out onto the road. A quick look into the rearview mirror confirmed that Zach Colby was right behind her.

A frown creased her forehead as she focused on the highway ahead, the swish of the windshield wipers loud in the silence.

It was disconcerting to learn that the big, intimidating rancher was her new neighbor. She wasn't sure if he was angry to learn that Aaron Hall was dead, or to discover that she was going to have Aaron's child. She was absolutely sure, however, that it had been fury that had blazed at her out of his ice blue eyes before he'd gone distant and abrupt and hustled her out of his truck.

The snow continued to fall from gray skies, the wind sending it swirling across the pavement, while the white flakes piled ever thicker in the pastures and tilled fields that lined the road until the pale yellow of dried prairie grass and the black of turned earth was obliterated by a white blanket.

CeCe reached the cluster of buildings that made up the small town of Butte Creek and quickly left them behind as she headed farther west. She felt as if she'd been driving for hours before she finally heard the truck's horn sound behind her.

She braked carefully, slowing to turn off the highway onto a lane, its entrance marked by a large black rural mailbox mounted at chest level atop a weathered post.

The snow lay deeper along the narrow lane, unbroken by the passage of vehicles. Behind her, the horn blared again and she glanced into her rearview mirror to see the pickup moving to the left to pass her. The vehicle pulled in front of her, its bigger truck tires crunching easily through the several inches of snow, and CeCe steered her little car into their packed-down tracks.

She was so focused on steering her car that it wasn't until Zach swung in a wide circle and braked to a stop that she realized they'd reached their destination.

It was difficult to see much of her new home through the white curtain of falling snow, but the dark bulk that loomed ahead of her was unmistakably a house.

She switched off the engine and set the brake, pushed open the door and slid out from beneath the wheel. The cold air hit her with frigid force, wind-driven snowflakes striking the exposed skin of her face with the impact of tiny icy pellets.

Zach met her before she'd gone more than a few steps and took her arm, his broad body shielding her from the wind as they hurried down a sidewalk and up three shallow steps where the overhang on the porch protected them from the snow and blocked the worst of the wind.

Zach rattled the doorknob, but the door didn't budge. "Looks like it's locked."

"I've got a key." CeCe selected a brass key from several on a ring and handed the jingling collection to him.

Zach scowled at the subtle proof that she had a right to reside in the house. The brass key slid smoothly into the lock, the door opening inward, and he stepped back to let CeCe enter ahead of him.

He'd never been inside this house in his life, and he wasn't eager to enter it now. Thirty-six years of being unwelcome made him hesitate before he stepped across the threshold.

Except for the lack of wind and snow, the inside of the house was barely warmer than the outside. Beside him, CeCe hugged her midsection and shivered.

"Gosh, it's cold in here," she exclaimed as she moved down the short hall, pausing to peer through a doorway at a long living room.

Zach flipped the switch beside the front door and light flooded the hallway. "The electricity's on," he commented.

"Thank goodness," CeCe responded, glancing over her shoulder at him. The brim of his hat shadowed his face, his features sculptured and strong in the bright overhead light. His broad-shouldered body and long legs were overwhelmingly male, and she shivered again, this time not from the cold. "I wrote to the power company several weeks ago and asked them to reconnect, but didn't get a response."

"What about the heat? Did you contact the oil company about the furnace?"

"Yes, and they promised to get the key from Aaron's attorney and check it for me."

Zach felt the familiar tightening of muscles at the mention of his half brother's name. He forced the feeling away, his glance sweeping searchingly over the walls of the hallway before he stepped across the threshold of the living room. "There must be a thermostat around here someplace—there it is."

He adjusted the temperature higher, relieved when he heard a click, and moments later the reassuring rumble of the heating unit.

"I'll bring your bags in," he said, turning to his new neighbor. She stood in the doorway, watching him, her eyes dark and unfathomable; she stepped back into the hallway as he approached.

"I'll help," she said firmly.

"No," he said just as firmly. "You stay here. It's too damn cold out there."

CeCe didn't argue. She had a feeling that very few people argued with the big man. Instead, she walked down the hallway away from him and pushed open doors, exploring. She found a square, old-fashioned kitchen with a pantry off one side, a large bathroom with tub and shower, a dining room and a big bedroom.

The rooms were dusty with disuse, the furniture well worn and comfortable-looking. CeCe walked back down the hall from the bedroom just as Zach shouldered his way through the front door with the last of her bags.

He dropped the cases next to the pile of boxes and bags that took up half the floor space of the modest living room and flicked a glance at the large cat carrier. The annoyed rumble coming from the carrier was loud in the quiet room.

"Big cat," he commented.

CeCe chuckled. "He's huge, isn't he? I think I'll leave Angus in his carrier until he settles down. He's not too happy with me—he hates riding in the car. He was an alleycat in Seattle before he adopted me. I think he might have been hit by a car in one of his past nine lives."

The smile that lit her face and turned her gray eyes dark with amusement hit Zach straight in the solar plexus. The throaty chuckle sent shivers of reaction chasing across his skin as surely as if she'd leaned into him and trailed her fingers up his thigh.

He yanked his gaze away from her face. "I have to go."

He strode out of the room.

CeCe stared at the empty doorway for one surprised second before she hurried after him. "Thank you for everything," she said.

He paused with his hand on the doorknob and looked over his shoulder at her. "When I was bringing in your bags, I noticed you'd packed a box of food. Do you need anything else?'' he asked reluctantly.

"No, thank you," she assured him. "I'm sure I'll be fine."

"Somebody will drop by tomorrow to check in on you," he said. "This weather may keep you housebound for a few days, so if you need anything just let us know."

"Thank you." She smiled at him, relieved. She was unwilling to admit, even to herself, that she was feeling a little intimidated by the ferocity of the storm and the isolation of her surroundings. Uncommunicative as Zach Colby was, and though his brusqueness bordered on rude, it was comforting that she knew at least one person in this new place. *Even if that one person is an incredibly sexy man who makes my obviously brainless, hormone-driven body go haywire,* she thought wryly.

CeCe stood at the living-room window, huddled for warmth in her heavy coat, her arms wrapped around her midriff in an effort to generate heat, and watched Zach's truck disappear down the snow-covered lane. She remained there long after his brake lights had blinked on and off at the end of the lane before he turned onto the highway, reluctant to leave the island of toasty air blowing from a floor vent beneath her feet. At last, the house warmed to the point where she no longer shivered, and she left her warm little oasis above the vent.

Her movement drew an irritated growl from the carrier.

"All right, Angus." CeCe knelt in front of the carrier and unfastened the latch to swing open the heavy wire door. "Come on out and take a look at your new home."

The big orange-and-white-striped tomcat leaped out of the carrier and halted immediately, whiskers twitching, ears swiveling as he surveyed his new territory.

CeCe ran a soothing palm over his head and down the length of his arched back and stiffly upright tail. "I'm glad I have you for company, Angus. I have a feeling it's going to get lonesome around here. It's just you, me, baby and the snow."

Angus looked up at her, his huge golden eyes glowing with interest, a purr rumbling in his chest.

The feel of the cat's soft fur and warm body was reassuring. CeCe sighed, gave Angus a final pat and pushed herself upright.

"I'm worn out from all the driving. What do you say we unpack some food and eat before we tackle making up the bed for tonight?"

Angus rumbled his approval, climbing atop a suitcase to watch while she shifted bags until she found the box of foodstuffs she'd packed in Seattle.

"Here we are." She pulled out a package of tea bags, a can of soup, tuna, canned milk, butter and bread. "You're eating fish tonight, my friend. Are you in the mood for tuna?"

Angus poked an inquisitive nose into the box, sniffing the contents. When CeCe stood and headed for the kitchen, the big cat quickly deserted the boxes and hurried after her.

The laboring furnace had pushed warm air throughout the house, making the temperature in the kitchen comfortable. CeCe dumped her armful of supplies on the counter by the sink, shrugged out of her heavy green jacket and hung it over the back of a nearby chair.

Angus was winding his furry body around her ankles, his rumbling purr growing louder by the minute.

"Poor baby, you're starving, aren't you?" CeCe pulled open drawers until she found a can opener. She opened the can of tuna, upended it in a small plastic bowl and set it on the floor. Angus immediately deserted her ankles and began to lap eagerly at the fish. He barely glanced up when she set a bowl of water beside the tuna.

By the time CeCe rummaged in the cabinets to locate pans, teakettle, dishes and utensils, heated her soup and brewed a mug of black tea, the view outside the kitchen window was completely dark. Night had fallen, obscuring what little could be seen of the ranch buildings through the snow.

"Maybe tomorrow we'll be able to look around outside, Angus." She sipped her tea, her gaze leaving the darkened window to rove around the outmoded kitchen. A frown slowly wrinkled her forehead. "That's odd." She pushed aside her empty soup bowl and rose. Carrying her mug, she left the kitchen and wandered down the hall, once again peering into the bedroom, bath and dining room before halting in the middle of the living room.

"I could have sworn that Aaron told me this house was only ten years old. Yes, I'm sure he did. He said his father built it for his mother for their twentieth anniversary.'' Her gaze moved consideringly over the room, registering the solid, square lines typical of 1950s architecture. "This house looks more like it was built during the forties or fifties—unless his mother purposely wanted it to look older."

Even the furniture was old-fashioned. The dark blue sofa and matching overstuffed chair were bulky, with wide, rolled arms and medium-high backs. The small table between sofa and chair was dark walnut with only a Tiffany-style lamp atop its dust-layered surface. It was a puzzle, but CeCe's tired brain couldn't come up with a clear solution.

She shrugged and bent over a box to pull out sheets and blankets, deciding to continue her unpacking. Juggling her tea and the nose-high stack of bedding, she made her way down the hall to the bedroom, followed by Angus. Here, too, the furniture was strangely old-fashioned, but the bed had a firm mattress and box spring. And by the time CeCe crawled between the sheets, she didn't care why Aaron's description of the house didn't match the reality.

She yawned once, shifted her feet beneath the blanket and Angus's weight on the covering quilt, and promptly fell asleep. Her dreams were haunted by a tall, blond cowboy with pale blue eyes.

Have I done the right thing?
Cradling her third mugful of morning decaf coffee in her hands, CeCe stood in the living room, staring out the wide, plate-glass window at the snow-covered landscape.

The snow had stopped falling sometime during the night, but the morning sky was overcast, gray and threatening. Her little blue car wore a blanket of white, as did the roofs of a large barn and several outbuildings that stood at the far edge of the snowy, large farm lot. The acre of white-covered lawn surrounding the house was enclosed by a fence, the bushes and trees within its lines shrouded in snow, while tiny top hats of pristine white capped the fence posts.

Not a creature stirred, not at the barns and not in the fields that stretched away from the small cluster of buildings. Nor could CeCe see any other buildings on the horizon. She might have been the only human alive, surrounded as she was by the vast expanse of land that climbed sharply into tall buttes to the north of the house, and dipped and rolled gently away to the south, the empty acres broken only by the fence lines etched in sharp black against the white snow.

Have I done the right thing? she asked herself again. Although she still stared out the window, her thoughts were far away in Seattle, ten months before.

She'd just celebrated her thirty-first birthday and her biological clock was ticking loudly—had been doing so, in fact, ever since she'd turned twenty-eight. After a short engagement in her early twenties that ended badly, she had no wish for a husband, but she desperately wanted a child. She'd been considering options and had even contacted an adoption agency.

Then she met Aaron Hall.

He'd rented the apartment next to hers several months before, but she'd rarely seen him. That changed, however, when she came home after work one evening and found him leaning weakly against the wall next to his door, clearly ill. Too exhausted and shaky to find the lock with his key, he was grateful for CeCe's help.

She continued to look in on him occasionally, and over the next six months they became casual friends. She learned that he was a rancher from Montana and that he was in Seattle to undergo treatment for lung cancer at the famed Fred Hutchinson Clinic.

Shortly after meeting CeCe, Aaron confided to her that the doctors weren't optimistic about his recovery. When he discovered that CeCe was considering adopting a child, he asked her to marry him and have his child, instead.

She was taken aback by his suggestion, but he quickly explained that he had donated sperm long before he became ill. The doctors had assured him that his particular type of cancer was caused by his cigarette smoking, not by a genetic predisposition to the disease. He was unmarried and without heirs. A sexual relationship was impossible due to his illness, but he wanted a child of his own to inherit his ranch.

In return for CeCe's agreement to have a medically induced pregnancy and to raise the child in Montana, Aaron offered to leave the ranch and all of his assets to her for their child.

At first she refused, but Aaron didn't give up. Eventually he persuaded her that although his proposal might sound outlandish at first hearing, the truth was that it benefited both of them. He could die in peace, knowing that he would have a child to inherit his land; she would have the baby she badly wanted, without bearing the prohibitive medical costs of insemination herself, without the long wait that was probable should she attempt to adopt and without the encumbrance of an unwanted man in her life if she decided to become pregnant in the conventional way.

Finally she agreed. The necessary medical information was exchanged, documents were drawn up, the marriage ceremony completed, and in late July, the medical procedure was a success. CeCe was pregnant—wonderfully, joyously pregnant. Her parents were concerned but supportive. Aaron seemed more grimly satisfied than elated, but she put down his lack of joy to his swiftly deteriorating health.

Within two and a half months, the man she hardly knew, but who had given her the child she so desperately wanted, had passed away. Per their agreement, CeCe arranged for his burial in Butte Creek but didn't attend. By November she had quit her job, closed up her apartment, loaded her car with her computer, her suitcases and her cat, arranged to have the rest of her belongings shipped, said a tearful goodbye to her parents and sister and left Seattle for Montana.

She still wasn't sure she'd done the right thing by transplanting herself and her unborn child to Montana. She was, however, absolutely, positively certain that becoming pregnant was right and that she wanted the baby that resided, safe, warm and protected, within her body.

The rumble of an engine interrupted her thoughts and she glanced down the lane; an unfamiliar truck with a snow-blade attached to the front was moving slowly toward the house, scraping the white drifts from the gravel lane.

Uneasy anticipation swirled inside her as she watched the truck draw nearer. If the driver was Zach Colby, she wasn't sure she wanted to see him. She wasn't ready to deal with the uneasy stirring of desire she felt when he was near. The man made her uncomfortable. Even with her fiancé all those years ago, she'd never felt quite that same primal reaction; it was embarrassing that her body would betray her, especially now, when she was pregnant.

Maybe that's what's causing it, she thought with sudden insight. *The prenatal books I read said that an increased level in sex drive is normal for some pregnant women.*

Relieved at the probability that she was dealing with normal side effects of her pregnancy, CeCe smiled brilliantly and lifted a hand to wave at the truck. The driver lifted a hand in response before he swung the vehicle in a large circle in front of the house, piling the snow on one side. The truck rumbled to a stop just beyond CeCe's little blue car and the driver shoved open the door and jumped down, shovel in hand. She was relieved to see it wasn't Zach.

CeCe watched the older man begin to shift snow away from the tires of her car before she slipped on her jacket, pulled her knit cap over her loose hair and stepped onto the porch.

Angus slipped through the door at her heels, halting at the top of the steps, nose twitching, to survey the frosty surroundings.

"Hello there."

The lanky man shoveling snow looked up, a slow grin curving his mouth. "Mornin'," he replied. He shoved his battered gray cowboy hat back on his head and ambled toward her.

His hair was snow-white beneath the hat, his jeans-covered legs slightly bowed. The bulky, thigh-length coat he wore reminded CeCe of the rough-cut suede jacket Zach had been wearing yesterday.

"You must be our new neighbor." He paused at the bottom of the steps and looked up at her.

"I'm Cecelia Hawkins. CeCe." She held out her hand, a smile curving her mouth in response to the twinkle in the older man's bright blue eyes.

"Pleased to meet you, Ms. Hawkins." He pulled off his glove and shook her hand. "I'm Charlie Allen. Zach asked me to plow your lane this morning."

"That's awfully nice of you—and him." CeCe fixed him with a curious gaze. "Do you work for Zach?"

"Nah." Charlie gestured toward the south. "My partner Murphy Redman and I have a place south of you—we live on the Hightower spread. But we swap work with Zach. He and the Hightower boys are about as close to family as Murphy and I have."

"Oh, I see." CeCe didn't exactly, but she was grateful that the rancher hadn't forgotten her. She glanced past Charlie at the plowed lane and then at the sky. "Do you suppose it will snow again today? I need to go to town, but I don't want to get caught on the road in another snowstorm."

"I'd give it a few days, if I were you," Charlie

replied. He tilted his head back and scanned the horizon. "From the looks of that sky, we're liable to get more snow before the day's over." He looked back at her. "Is it an emergency? Do you have to get to town today?"

"No." She shook her head. "I just wanted to run a few errands."

"You're sure you're okay? Got enough food? The furnace is working all right?"

"I'm fine. The house is warm and I brought enough groceries with me to last a while."

"That reminds me..." Charlie smacked his hand against his thigh and hurried off down the sidewalk. "Zach told me to give you this," he called over his shoulder. The rest of his words were muffled as he leaned inside the cab of the truck to pluck something off the seat. "...in case you need to get ahold of one of us for any reason." He walked back to her and held out a cellular phone and a slim telephone book. "He said to keep it until you get your phone line connected."

"How thoughtful!" Delight colored her tone. CeCe clutched the phone and the soft-covered book and smiled brilliantly at the older cowboy. He stared at her and blinked slowly before an answering grin turned up the corners of his mouth.

"I guess that means you like it?" he said drolly.

"I guess you're right," she said, laughing self-consciously. "I was feeling a little isolated."

"Yeah." His gaze traveled over the snow-covered barn and the bare fields and buttes beyond. "It can get a little quiet around here—especially if you're used to living in town.''

"Mmm," CeCe murmured in agreement.

"I better get goin'. I've got Josh and Sarah's lane to plow yet this mornin'. They're nice folks. You'll probably be meetin' them soon 'cause they're friends of Zach.'' He turned back to her and held out a gnarled, callused hand. "Well, it was a pleasure to meet you, Ms. Hawkins. You be sure to call now, if there's anything we can do to help you get settled.''

"Thank you, Charlie." CeCe placed her hand in his and was rewarded with a firm, warm handshake. "And I will call if I need anything.''

"Good, you do that. So long.''

CeCe stood on the cold porch, watching him back the truck and turn to go down the lane. He waved and she answered with a lift of her hand before she shivered and went inside the house.

Charlie's prediction came true. The afternoon brought snow, and over the next two days the white flakes swirled down day and night. When CeCe woke on the third day to find sunshine and clear skies, she was delighted. Once again, she sipped her morning coffee and kept watch out the window for Charlie.

At last, she was rewarded by the rumble of the big truck, the heavy metal wings of the plow clearing a swath up the snowy lane. The truck turned in a wide circle and braked to a halt in front of the house.

But it wasn't Charlie Allen who swung down from the high cab. It was Zach Colby.

Chapter Two

Zach was halfway up the snowy sidewalk when CeCe Hawkins stepped out onto the porch.

He halted abruptly, stopped as surely as if he'd walked into a brick wall. The weak sunlight gleamed off streaks of gold in the thick fall of her dark hair. His gaze flicked quickly from the crown of her head to her toes and back up again, taking in the curves and slim lines of her body in one swift, assessing glance. She hadn't fastened her jacket and it hung open, revealing a thigh-length red sweater over narrow-legged black jeans. Try as he might, he couldn't detect the roundness of pregnancy.

I wonder when the baby's due.

A brief telephone conversation with the attorney for the Hall estate on the morning after he'd left CeCe had netted him the information that she and Aaron had married in early July.

And this is only November, so it's possible that she's only a few months pregnant.

Once again, the knowledge that CeCe Hawkins had belonged to Aaron hit Zach with raw force, reminding him that the widow was off limits. *Regardless of my body's reaction to her,* he told himself grimly, *my head knows that she's the last woman I want in my life.*

Unfortunately, given the details of Kenneth Hall's will, and my obligation to that baby she's carrying, that's probably going to be impossible.

"Good morning." CeCe paused at the top of the porch steps, eyeing the silent rancher warily. She couldn't decipher his expression, but he responded to her greeting by moving forward, his long strides closing the distance to the bottom of the steps with swift ease.

"Morning." He halted and looked up at her. "I picked up your tire at the garage this morning. Jake found a nail puncture and repaired it. If you'll give me your keys, I'll get the jack out of your car trunk and switch the tires back."

"Oh, thank you." CeCe gave him a tentative smile, but he didn't return it. The lines of his face remained remote. "My keys are inside—I'll be right back."

She turned and disappeared into the house, reappearing moments later.

"Here they are."

Before Zach could step away, CeCe descended the stairs and held out a ring of keys. He automatically cupped his palm and she dropped the cluster of metal into his hand. Her fingertips brushed his and he felt the jolt of electricity down to his toes.

CeCe nearly jumped at the sizzle of awareness that arced from his fingers to hers. Her gaze shot swiftly up to his, but she found no sign of awareness on his still features; she stepped back, widening the space between his body and hers.

"Do you think the storm is over?" She half turned from him, self-consciously tucking a strand of hair behind her ear.

"For today," Zach answered briefly, his gaze narrowing as he scanned the blue skies and clear horizon.

"Good. I need to run some errands in town," she commented. "Do you think the roads are safe?"

"Sure." Zach nodded in confirmation. "The county snowplows were out early this morning and cleared all the main roads. You shouldn't have any problem driving to Butte Creek as soon as I replace the good snow tire on your car."

"That's great." She sighed with relief.

Zach didn't miss her reaction. "It shouldn't take me more than a few minutes to change the tire. You suffering from cabin fever already?"

There was a cynical edge to his deep voice and CeCe stiffened, her eyes narrowing as she turned to face him. His eyes were remote and noncommittal, his hard features reflecting neither derision nor judgment as he waited for her answer.

"No," she said abruptly. This time, one blond eyebrow lifted slightly, and though his lips didn't move, amusement lurked in his ice blue eyes. "Well, maybe a little," she admitted reluctantly.

"Hmm." A swift, unbidden smile curved his mouth. "In that case, I'd better hurry and get your tire changed."

He touched the brim of his hat and turned. Speechless, CeCe stared at his broad back as he walked away from her, stunned by the impact of that brief smile and the transformation of his face from austere gruffness to devastating handsomeness.

"Oh my goodness," she breathed softly, the whispered words puffing little clouds into the cold air. "That man is lethal."

Shaking her head at her reaction to the rancher, she hurried into the house.

She was still making out a grocery list when Zach knocked on her front door. Pencil in hand, she pulled open the door and bent swiftly to catch Angus as he darted between her legs.

"Hey, you can't go outside," she protested. She straightened, cradling the heavy orange-and-white tomcat in her arms. "Sorry. If I let him roam outside, heaven knows when he'll come back, and I want him safe in the house while I'm in town."

Bemused at the vivid picture she made holding the big cat, Zach stared at her for a silent moment before he remembered why he came to her door.

"I...uh..." He paused and cleared his throat. "I changed the tire and started your car. The engine was a little grumpy, so you might think about parking it inside the machine shop from now on to keep it out of the weather."

"All right, I will. Thank you."

He nodded, touched the brim of his hat in brief, silent farewell, and left the porch. CeCe watched him stride down the walk and across the lot to his truck before she shivered with cold and turned back into the house.

"That man doesn't talk much, Angus," she commented as she set the large cat down on the floor.

"But then, a man who looks as good as he does in boots and jeans doesn't really have to say much. I bet I'm not the only woman whose heart goes crazy when he smiles at her."

CeCe eased her car into a parking space in front of the Butte Creek National Bank, switched off the engine and breathed a sigh of relief.

I wonder how long it will be before I'm comfortable driving on snow-covered roads?

Gathering up her purse, she thrust open the door and slipped out from beneath the wheel. The snow crunched beneath her boots, the air crisp and cold in her lungs. She shut the car door and stepped up on the sidewalk, glancing around to get her bearings. Directly in front of her was the faded brick facade of the bank. The matching redbrick building next door had a large front window overlooking the sidewalk. Distinguished gold letters, edged in black, scrolled their way across its surface.

"Henry Wallace, Attorney-at-Law," she read aloud. *Easy enough to find,* she thought with satisfaction.

The small bell attached to the door jangled musically when CeCe stepped across the threshold and into the reception area of the lawyer's office. The gray-haired secretary seated behind a desk to CeCe's right looked up and smiled politely.

CeCe started across the room but halted abruptly when an inner door opened and Zach Colby appeared. He paused in midstride, his gaze flicking swiftly down her body. Startled, trapped by the hot awareness that blazed in his eyes, she stared at him. His searing glance moved upward, and CeCe's breath caught in her throat. His gaze paused, lingering for a split second on her midsection, his eyes narrowing before he met hers once again.

The ice blue depths were once again cool and remote. CeCe decided she must have imagined the sizzle of heat that she'd felt between them, and struggled to manage a pleasant smile.

"Hello, Zach."

"Ms. Hawkins." Zach nodded a brief acknowledgment and stepped into the room, half turning to glance at the man behind him. "Henry, this is Cecelia Hawkins. Ms. Hawkins—Henry Wallace."

CeCe glanced from Zach to the shorter, balding man in time to see the attorney's eyes widen in surprise behind his glasses before he smiled and nodded.

"Good morning, Ms. Hawkins. It's a pleasure to finally meet you."

"Likewise, Mr. Wallace." CeCe held out her hand and the attorney clasped it firmly.

"Thanks for your time, Henry," Zach said abruptly. "I'll be in touch."

"Certainly, Zach." The attorney shook Zach's hand. "You do that."

Zach nodded at CeCe and left the reception area. The door closed behind his broad back, the bell jingling once again, and she realized she was once more standing motionless, staring after him.

"Won't you step into my office, Ms. Hawkins?"

The attorney's invitation drew her attention away from the empty doorway.

"Certainly." CeCe moved past him and into the spacious inner room. Law books filled glass-fronted walnut cases, and forest green carpeting set off dark-paneled walls.

"Can I get you some coffee? Tea, maybe?"

She glanced over her shoulder at him. "No, thank you."

"Very well." He closed the door behind him and gestured to the two comfortable, upholstered armchairs arranged in front of a large cherry-wood desk. "Please, have a seat."

CeCe complied and waited while he rounded the desk and sat. The heavy swivel desk chair creaked as it took his weight.

"I'm glad you came in today." He leaned forward, resting his folded hands atop the desk's blotter. "I hope you had a safe trip from Seattle."

"I did, except for the last fifty miles or so when it snowed. I wanted to stop in and introduce myself," CeCe responded. "As you know, I'll be living at Aaron's ranch, should you need to contact me regarding his estate."

"Ah, yes," Henry fidgeted, shuffling papers as if searching for something. "Aaron Hall's estate."

CeCe waited for a long moment, but he didn't say anything further.

"Is there a problem?" she asked finally, eyeing his nervous movements.

The attorney's fingers stilled and he peered over his glasses at her, a worried frown creasing his forehead. "I hope not, but I have some concerns that your husband may have been less than truthful with you about the details of the Hall estate."

CeCe stiffened and sat straighter in her chair. "What do you mean—less than truthful?"

"I suspect that Aaron told you that the Hall ranch was his to dispose of. It's not."

CeCe was stunned.

"It's not?" she said slowly, certain she must have misunderstood him.

"No, I'm afraid it's not." The attorney sighed and thrust his fingers through his hair before he pulled a file folder from the stack atop his desk and flipped it open. "The Hall estate is rather complicated," he said. "Aaron's father, Kenneth Hall, left a will that granted Aaron the use of the land and buildings during his lifetime, but not the right to sell or mortgage the property—nor to bequeath the estate to anyone. More specifically, Kenneth Hall left the family's land and trust accounts to Aaron's half brother. However, if Aaron had children, then one-half of the estate was to go to those children. If anything happened to Aaron while the child or children were minors, his half brother would be named as trustee of the children's portion of the estate and manager of the entire ranch until the eldest child reached the age of twenty-five.''

Dazed, CeCe could only stare at the attorney. Aaron had told her none of this.

''I don't understand. When we married, Aaron signed documents that named me as his beneficiary. Are you saying that they're useless?'' she demanded incredulously.

''I'm saying that Aaron Hall didn't have the legal right to draw up a last will and testament leaving the Hall ranch and trust accounts to you. However,'' he went on, ''any children Aaron fathered have the right to claim one-half of the ranch and the trust. It's my understanding from your correspondence that you're expecting a child, is that correct?''

''Yes.'' CeCe nodded slowly, still trying to absorb the impact of his words. ''I wish I'd known this before I quit my job, packed up my life and moved all this way,'' she murmured aloud. She rubbed her temple where a headache was beginning to throb. ''Why didn't you write and explain this when I sent you a letter introducing myself when Aaron died? It must have been clear that I planned to move here.''

''It was,'' the attorney said. ''But your letter indicated that you and your late husband had agreed that you would raise his child here in Butte Creek on the family ranch. Through your child, you have a home and income here. Although you personally do not own the Hall ranch, your child does own half of it.''

For the first time, CeCe registered the fact that the attorney had twice mentioned a half brother. ''Who owns the other half?'' she asked.

"Zach Colby."

Oh, no! Not him! Dismay filled CeCe. Zach Colby had already demonstrated his low opinion of her ability to take care of herself. She'd observed firsthand his high-handed tactics, and she strongly suspected that he would try to run her child's life—and hers— if she let him. Besides, the rancher was too blatantly male, too intimidating, and she was entirely too aware of him.

"Aaron never mentioned that he had a brother."

"Half brother." Mr. Wallace corrected her gently.

CeCe frowned. "I'm positive Aaron told me that his parents were married a very long time. Was his mother married to someone else before her marriage to Aaron's father?"

"Not as far as I know." The attorney shifted in his seat and cleared his throat. "Zach Colby is Kenneth's son."

CeCe continued to stare at him without comprehension.

"Zach Colby and Aaron Hall are only a few months apart in age," Mr. Wallace said bluntly. "Kenneth Hall was married to Aaron's mother. Zach's mother is the daughter of a neighboring rancher."

Understanding dawned. CeCe shook her head slowly, disbelievingly. "So Aaron was the legitimate son, and Zach Colby was illegitimate." The attorney nodded in silent confirmation. "Why did Aaron's father write such a ridiculously Victorian will? Why didn't he simply divide the estate and leave half to each son?"

Henry Wallace sighed and pushed his eyeglasses higher on his nose. "I tried to talk him out of it, but he was determined. And," he went on, "given the past history of those two boys, I can't tell you that he was completely wrong."

"Past history?" CeCe asked. "What do you mean?"

"That ranch has been in the Hall family for generations. Kenneth wanted it to stay that way, but he had more than good cause to be concerned that if he split the ranch in two on his death, Aaron would gamble away his half of the estate and the land would be lost to Hall descendants forever."

"Aaron gambled?" CeCe was getting a very different version of Aaron Hall than the man she'd known in Seattle.

"Among other things, yes."

CeCe was afraid to ask what other things.

"If Aaron had a gambling problem, why didn't Mr. Hall leave the entire ranch to Zach Colby?"

"Kenneth would never have cut off Aaron entirely. Besides, there's been bad blood between Zach and Aaron for years. Gossip said Zach even divorced his wife because of Aaron. Heaven only knows what Aaron would have done if his father had left the ranch to Zach. As it was, Aaron exploded when the will was read. Those two boys hated each other."

CeCe shook her head in disbelief. *What have I got myself into?*

She's been in there for more than an hour. Zach's fingers tapped an impatient tattoo against the steering wheel of his pickup and he scowled through the windshield at the office across the street. *How long can it take Henry to tell her about the will?*

He doubted that Cecelia Hawkins was going to be happy with what the attorney had to tell her. He was none too happy with the situation himself, but Henry had already confirmed that Kenneth Hall's last will and testament was ironclad and unbreakable. He and the widow were stuck with each other.

The office door opened and he stiffened, his eyes narrowing over CeCe's slim figure as she stepped out onto the sidewalk, pulling the door shut behind her. She stood motionless, frowning at the street.

Zach watched her for a long moment, but she neither looked up nor moved, clearly deep in thought.

"Well, hell," he muttered resignedly. "I suppose I might as well get this over with."

He shoved the pickup door open and got out, waiting for a sedan to drive slowly past before he strode across the wide street.

"Ms. Hawkins."

The deep voice was unmistakably male and too familiar. Startled, CeCe looked up quickly. His black Stetson pulled low over his eyes, Zach Colby was the last person in the world she wanted to see.

"Mr. Colby," she said evenly.

Zach searched her face. Irritation and wariness darkened her eyes to stormy gray.

"I assume Henry explained the terms of Kenneth Hall's will," he said flatly.

It wasn't a question.

"You knew all along, didn't you? Why didn't you

say something when you picked me up on the high-way and I told you where I was going?'' CeCe de-manded.

"For all I knew, Aaron had found a way to break Kenneth's will,'' Zach answered tersely. "If he had, I didn't see any reason to tell you about the original will.''

"Well, you should have told me,'' CeCe snapped, brushing her hair back over her shoulder with quick, impatient fingers. "That will changes everything.''

"I don't see why.''

CeCe glared at him. He stared back impassively and her frustration with the situation inched upward another notch.

Zach read the hostility on her features and glanced around them. "The street is no place for this discus-sion,'' he told her, catching her elbow in one big palm. "Let's take this inside. We'll talk about it over coffee.''

"I don't drink anything that has caffeine after breakfast,'' CeCe told him, stubbornly refusing to move. "It's bad for the baby.''

"Fine,'' he said tersely. "You can have hot water if you want, but we're going inside where it's warm.'' His fingers closed firmly over her arm and he drew her with him into the restaurant two doors down from the bank.

Irritated beyond belief at the disruption of her well-laid plans for her child's future, CeCe reluctantly al-lowed him to usher her to a booth at the back of the restaurant. It wasn't until they'd shed their coats and the young waitress had taken their order and left them alone that he spoke.

"I know you're not happy about sharing the Hall ranch," he began abruptly. "Neither am I. But Henry tells me that there's no way to break the will. We're stuck with each other."

"How nice." CeCe wanted to reach across the table and shake him. After all her careful plans, it was inconceivable that this man had a measure of control over her child's life.

Zach ignored the hostile bite in her polite words. "Did Henry explain the financial conditions?"

"He told me that you were appointed trustee of *my* child's inheritance until she's twenty-five."

"She?" Diverted, Zach glanced swiftly downward, but CeCe's waist was hidden beneath the edge of the table. "You know it's a girl?"

"No," she responded reluctantly. "Not for sure. But I hope it's a little girl."

"Hmm." Zach was uneasy with the unexpected flash of curiosity he'd felt and deliberately returned to the subject of the will. "I asked Henry this morning for details about the trust fund. There's enough money for you to draw a monthly allowance over the winter. If you'll give me your account number, I'll stop at the bank before I leave town and make arrangements to have funds transferred the first of each month."

"I haven't opened an account here yet," she told him. "I'd planned to visit the bank after I saw Mr. Wallace. Besides, I have money of my own," she added. "I don't need to draw money from the estate."

Zach eyed the stubborn tilt of her chin. "What about expenses for the baby—doctors' bills, hospital?"

"They'll be covered by insurance," she responded shortly. "You don't have to concern yourself with my financial situation."

"The hell I don't," Zach snarled at her. "That will the old bastard left made me responsible for that baby you're carrying. Like it or not, you're stuck with me—and I'm stuck with you and the kid."

"Oh no you're not," CeCe snapped back, her cheeks heating with temper. "I don't want or need your interference in my life—or in my baby's life."

"Believe me, lady," Zach said in a clipped tone, "I'd rather be boiled in oil than get involved with you and that baby you're carrying. But I don't have any choice—and neither do you."

"People always have a choice," she said flatly. "Stay out of our lives. We'll get along just fine without you."

"Yeah, right," he said derisively. "You were doing real well with that flat tire in the snow."

"I'll learn to deal with the snow," she said tightly. "And with anything else I have to learn in order to live in Montana and raise my child here. *Without* your help."

Zach glared at the woman seated across the booth from him. The waitress chose that moment to appear, placing steaming mugs on the table in front of them. He bit back an acid retort and waited until the young woman left before speaking.

"Like it or not, there's no getting around the terms

of that will. I have to manage the ranch—your child's half along with mine. I may not like it, but I'll do it," he said grimly. He wished he could shed the responsibility, but the memory of his own childhood without a father wouldn't let him turn his back on his duty. "And like it or not, you'll have to cooperate. The kid will grow up on the ranch and I'll have to teach him—or her—how to manage the place so that when they're old enough to take over their half, they'll be ready."

Exasperated with the situation, CeCe wished she wasn't too mature to throw herself on the floor, drum her heels and scream with frustration. Whether he admitted it or not, Zach had to resent the fact that her child would take away half of an estate that he undoubtedly had expected to inherit in total. She refused to acknowledge an odd sense of hurt that he was so clearly annoyed at being forced to deal with her and the baby nestled under her heart. Nor did she want to consider the possibility that she'd been used by Aaron to hurt Zach.

"Just because you were drafted to serve as trustee of my child's financial affairs doesn't mean you're required to spend time with her. Or him," she said stiffly. "If your conscience demands you take an active part in her life, content yourself by sending flowers when she graduates from college."

Zach didn't agree that his role would be that easily accomplished, but it was clear that arguing with the stubborn widow was getting him nowhere. He abandoned the attempt for the moment and abruptly changed the subject. "I'll stop by in a day or two to check the house. No one's lived there for the last year and I want to make sure the roof is solid and the weather stripping around the windows and doors is secure.''

"All right," CeCe agreed reluctantly. She glanced at her watch. "Is there any further business we need to discuss? If not, I have several stops I need to make and I want to be home before dark."

"No, I think we've dealt with the basics—for the moment," Zach said shortly. She turned to pick up her gloves from the bench beside her. "Are you worried about driving on snow-covered roads?"

CeCe paused in the act of smoothing the leather gloves over her fingers and glanced up at him. A small frown pulled down his tawny eyebrows.

"Of course I am," she said calmly, tugging the gloves on firmly. "I'm not a complete fool, Mr. Colby, regardless of what you may believe."

"I didn't say I thought you were a fool," he muttered, his frown turning fiercer.

"No?" She arched an eyebrow at him in patent disbelief. "Perhaps you didn't actually say the words," she conceded. "But then, I'm not sure you needed to."

With that, she slid out of the booth and stood, her back to him. However, before she could take her heavy winter jacket from the coat hook attached to the booth's end post, Zach stood, too, reached around her and lifted it down. For one brief moment, she was surrounded by him, his chest pressed against her shoulder blades. She drew a deep, startled breath and caught the scent of aftershave and crisp fresh air, underlaid with the unique male scent that she knew instinctively was Zach's alone. He stepped back, releasing her from the spell that held her immobile.

Her heart pounding, she turned quickly and looked up at him. He stood patiently, holding her coat, and once again she couldn't read the flash of emotion in his cool eyes. Without comment, she turned away from him and slipped her arms into the jacket. His hands didn't linger on her shoulders, and she caught up her purse from the table, stepping silently past him. She was vividly aware of him stalking behind her as she walked the length of the small restaurant.

She paused at the counter just inside the door, where a large, ornate, old-fashioned cash register held pride of place, and glanced back at him. "Did the waitress give us a bill?"

"No." Zach shoved a hand into his jeans pocket and drew out a roll of bills. CeCe pulled a wallet from her purse at the same moment. "I'm buying," he said flatly, and tossed a five-dollar bill down atop the counter.

CeCe opened her mouth to argue, but the black scowl on his handsome features gave her second thoughts. "Oh, all right," she said ungraciously as she shoved her wallet back into her purse. She glared at him. "Do you ever discuss matters, or do you always issue declarations and ultimatums?"

Startled, Zach stared down into her disgruntled features for a moment before he smiled. "I find it simplifies life to cut down arguing time."

"Hmmph." She frowned at him. His blue eyes twinkled with amusement, his teeth flashing white against tan skin. He was heartbreakingly handsome when he wasn't scowling. *And I'm sure he knows it,* she thought with irritation.

Without further comment, she turned, pushed open the door and stepped out onto the sidewalk.

The door swung closed behind them and Zach caught her arm, releasing her immediately when she paused and turned to look up at him.

"I have a couple of stops of my own to make before I head home," he said. "I'll wait for you and follow you home. How long do you think you'll be?"

"An hour or two," CeCe replied. "But you don't need to wait for me. I can find my way home."

"I'm sure you can," Zach said with exasperation. "But we're neighbors and we're going the same way. There's no reason for you to worry about driving on snow."

"I'm not *that* worried," CeCe lied without a single twinge of guilt. "And you are *not* responsible for me," she added firmly.

"Maybe not for you," he replied tersely. "But I am for that baby you're carrying."

Frustrated at his stubborn insistence, CeCe glared at the big rancher while she struggled to rein in her rising temper.

"Zach!"

The cheerful, feminine call stopped CeCe from uttering a scathing reply. A warm, welcoming smile lit Zach's austere features, his cool blue eyes softening with affection. CeCe ignored the stab of dismay at his reaction to the woman's voice and glanced over her shoulder.

A slim woman, her red-gold hair a riot of corkscrew curls that fell around her shoulders, walked toward them. A tall, handsome, black-haired man in boots, jeans and cowboy hat strode beside her, a chubby toddler perched on his arm. A little boy, his deep blue eyes sparkling beneath a shock of black hair, ran ahead of them.

"Unca Zach!"

"Hey, Wayne."

The boy launched himself at Zach when he was still several feet away, and Zach laughed, easily catching the sturdy body and swinging him up to sit on his shoulder.

Zach grunted and pretended to stagger under the little boy's weight. "Good grief, you weigh a ton! What's your mama been feedin' you—rocks?"

"No." The little boy chortled and wrapped his arms tightly around Zach's neck. "Oatmeal and chocolate chip cookies."

"A lethal combination," his mother said dryly, smiling at CeCe.

Zach glanced down at CeCe. "Ms. Hawkins, I'd like you to meet Jennifer and Lucas Hightower, and their sons, Wayne and Steve. They have a spread south of yours."

"Ah, so we're neighbors?" CeCe returned the woman's warm smile.

"How terrific!" Jennifer Hightower exclaimed with delight. "We need more women in the county. As you can see, I'm outnumbered by men."

The toddler chose that moment to reach for his

mother, and his father caught him just in time to keep him from diving headfirst toward the sidewalk.

Jennifer laughed and took the red-cheeked little boy from his father's arms, perching him on her hip. "Are you visiting family here?"

"No." CeCe shook her head, impressed by the ease with which the slim woman dealt with the squirming little boy. "I'm living at Aaron Hall's ranch."

An abrupt silence fell over the group. Lucas's gaze sharpened; Jennifer's gold eyes lit with curiosity and concern before moving swiftly from Zach's impassive face to CeCe's.

Obviously, the two knew something of the circumstances surrounding the ranch and their friend Zach, CeCe mused. Just as obviously, they wondered where she fit in.

"I'm Aaron's widow," CeCe said in a carefully neutral voice. "I'll be staying at the Hall ranch for a while."

Zach glanced swiftly at her, a frown growing. "A long while," he said authoritatively.

CeCe shrugged. "Perhaps."

"I'm sorry to hear about the loss of your husband. However, I'm delighted to have another woman close enough to visit," Jennifer interjected. "I hope you stay in Butte Creek for a long time."

Warmth flooded CeCe. Jennifer's words were immensely reassuring, especially after the shock of learning the truth about Aaron's will and the role that Zach Colby would play in her baby's life.

"I'm glad you live near. I'm afraid Butte Creek is a drastic change from Seattle. And the snow..."

"Seattle! You moved here from Seattle?"

"Yes," CeCe answered.

"I lived in Seattle before I moved to Montana!" Jennifer exclaimed.

"Really?" CeCe laughed with delight. "What a small world."

"Mommy. Mommy!" The toddler perched on Jennifer's hip patted her cheek insistently.

"What is it, Stevie?"

"Want chocolate."

"Me, too!" Wayne chimed in.

"Uh-oh." Jennifer glanced apologetically at CeCe. "I'm afraid we have to feed these two. Listen, we're in the phone book. Call me—or I'll call you."

"I will." CeCe laughed when Stevie tugged impatiently on a handful of his mother's hair.

"Come here, you little monster," Lucas growled threateningly, his mild tone without heat. "You're not supposed to pull your mother's hair."

The little boy went willingly into his daddy's arms, chattering happily.

"Nice to meet you, Ms. Hawkins." Lucas nodded at CeCe and shot Zach an unreadable look. "Drop by our place soon, Zach. Josh and I have a colt we want you to look at."

"All right. I'll do that," Zach replied. He swung Wayne to his feet and watched as Jennifer caught his hand. "Take it easy on your mom, slugger."

"Okay." Wayne flashed him a sunny smile and

gifted CeCe with the same sweet grin. "Bye, Ms. 'awkins."

"Bye, Wayne."

The quartet disappeared into the restaurant and Zach looked down at CeCe.

"I'll meet you back here in an hour or two, if that gives you enough time."

CeCe stared at him silently before sighing deeply, giving up the battle. "Two hours would be better."

"All right. Two hours it is."

He touched his hat in a polite goodbye and strode across the street to climb into his truck.

CeCe squared her shoulders and walked swiftly, purposefully, the short distance down the sidewalk to the bank. "Just as soon as I can, I've got to figure out a way to convince that man that he can't follow me around and guard me," she muttered.

It took her longer than two hours to complete her errands, including a stop at the grocery store to stock her pantry shelves with staples, but Zach was waiting when she reached the cafe. Dusk had fallen by the time she turned off the highway into the lane that led to her house.

To her surprise, Zach followed her down the lane, pulling up behind her when she parked in front of the house. By the time she switched off the engine and gathered up her purse, he was opening her door, waiting patiently for her to step out.

"I'll carry your groceries inside," he said in response to the questioning look she gave him.

"You don't have to," she began. "I can——"

"I know you can. And I know I don't have to," he interrupted. "You're tired, and with two of us carrying bags, you'll be done that much faster and sitting inside where it's warm."

CeCe would have argued, but he was right. The pregnancy sapped her strength, and lately she'd been taking naps in the afternoon. She hadn't rested today, and weariness dragged at her as early dusk threw shadows over the cold landscape.

"All right," she capitulated.

Prepared to argue, Zach was taken aback by her abrupt surrender. "That's it?" he asked in surprise. "No argument?"

CeCe shot him a wry, weary look. "I'm too tired to argue. Besides, I try very hard not to cut off my nose to spite my own face. I'll fight with you over your irritating habit of ordering me around later, when I'm not so exhausted."

"Well, I'll be damned." Zach shoved his Stetson back on his head and eyed her quizzically. "A reasonable woman. Will wonders ever cease?"

"I'm warning you," she replied. "Just as soon as I have a nap, we're going to have a talk about this ridiculous compulsion you have to order me around."

Zach chuckled, the sound a deep rumble of genuine amusement in the cold air.

"Yes, ma'am."

He saluted her and followed her to the back of the car. As soon as she fitted the key into the lock and the trunk opened, he picked up three heavy grocery bags and set off up the sidewalk to the house. By the time CeCe reached the porch with two lighter bags, he was returning.

"Don't lift anything heavy," he ordered her as he passed.

"Yes, General," she muttered.

By the time she dropped her purse and the bags on the countertop in the kitchen, Zach was back, four brown-paper grocery sacks in his arms. He set them down atop the table and glanced around the room.

"That's all the bags from the trunk. Anything else you need out of the car?"

"No."

"Then I'll put your car in the machine shop."

He turned on his heel and left the kitchen. CeCe stared after him for a moment.

"What happened to 'Would you like me to put your car in the machine shop?' " she muttered to herself.

She shrugged out of her heavy coat and hung it over the back of a kitchen chair. Pushing her sweater sleeves up to her elbows, she filled the teakettle and set it on the stove burner.

Angus appeared, stretching and yawning before he wound around her ankles, purring.

"Hi, big boy." CeCe bent to rub him gently between the ears. "Did you miss me?"

The big cat purred louder, pushing against her fingers.

"I missed you, too." CeCe straightened. "I think it's a little chilly in here. Maybe we should turn up the thermostat."

Followed by the orange-and-white cat, she left the

lamplit kitchen. She hurried down the dim hallway, turned right into the dark living room and walked straight into Zach.

"Oh!" Startled, she stumbled against him and clutched fistfuls of his flannel shirt, the backs of her hands tight against the solid muscles beneath.

Taken by surprise, Zach instinctively wrapped his arms around her, securing her slim body against the length of his. The hallway was dark, lit only by the spill of light from the kitchen door at the far end. CeCe tilted her head back and looked up at him, her gray eyes wide and startled.

Zach saw surprise turn to awareness and was instantly, hotly aware of the full curves of her breasts pressed against his chest and the slim thighs aligned with his.

He wanted her.

Of all the women in the world, why did she have to be the one to make him crazy?

Chapter Three

"Meow."

The plaintive yowl split the tense silence. A large, furry body butted against Zach's ankle with demanding insistence, jolting him back to reality. This wasn't just another woman in his arms. This was Aaron Hall's widow.

He forced his reluctant fingers to loosen their hold and stepped back, his hands loosely cupping her elbows to support her.

"You all right?" His voice was rusty, even to his own ears.

"Yes."

Her fingers released his shirt. He felt their trembling before they lost contact with his body, and the swift, fierce need to catch them, slip them inside the rough flannel and stroke their slim warmth against his bare skin slammed into him.

CeCe stepped back, freeing herself from Zach's loose clasp on her arms. She threaded unsteady fingers through her hair. "I'm sorry. I didn't see you."

"My fault. It's dark in here...I turned the thermostat up—I guess I should have turned a light on," he said gruffly.

"Oh. I, uh, was just on my way to do that—turn up the heat, that is." CeCe wrapped her arms around her waist.

"Yeah, well..." Zach hesitated. "I better get going," he said abruptly. "I've got stock to feed."

"Right." CeCe followed him the few steps to the door. "Good night."

"Good night." He paused on the porch and looked back at her. *Hell,* he thought with disgust, *I'll be damned if I'll apologize.* He tore his gaze away from the sight of her slim, curvy body framed in the doorway. "Get some sleep."

"Yes, sir."

He ignored the snap in her reply and strode down the sidewalk.

CeCe shivered and closed the door. But she couldn't resist pulling back the curtain to watch him climb into his truck and drive down the lane to the highway.

"Men," she muttered. "I don't need this, Angus. I'm three months pregnant—a happy circumstance that I've longed for, yearned for. I had my life beautifully organized before Zach Colby appeared. I do *not* need my pregnancy-crazy hormones giving me an attack of lust every time that man looks at me with those incredibly hot eyes.'' She groaned and turned away from the door. Muttering dire warnings to herself, she retreated down the hallway to the kitchen, Angus following companionably at her heels, chirping and purring in response to her voice. ''Besides, how much can I trust the man when my baby stands between him and one-half of this ranch? Even though he hasn't said so, he must resent me and my baby for taking it away from him.''

The teakettle was steaming, whistling merrily in the quiet of the kitchen.

''If I have to be in the same room with Zach, I'm just going to ignore him, Angus,'' she said as she crossed to the stove. ''And starting right now, I'm going to work very hard to smother the slightest trace of attraction.''

Angus chose that moment to cough loudly.

CeCe flashed him a warning look. The cat returned her glare with an innocent, feline blink of his wide golden eyes. ''Don't be such a critic. I'm having enough trouble believing this myself. I don't need any help, thank you very much.''

Angus meowed placatingly and tilted his head to the side.

She sighed. ''All right. I'll feed you. But try to be a little more supportive, okay?''

She opened the lower cabinet door where she stored the cat food and Angus rumbled his approval, his purr growing louder as she filled his dish.

Several miles away, Zach muttered as he broke apart hay bales and forked alfalfa from the barn loft into the stalls below.

"I'll be damned if I'll go near that woman again," he snarled, jabbing the pitchfork into another flake of hay. He could still feel the imprint of her body against his chest and thighs, seared indelibly into his skin with the heat generated when they touched.

"Maybe it's not the widow. Maybe I just need to get laid."

He gave brief thought to the always-willing divorcée in the next county that he visited on rare occasions, but just as quickly discarded the idea.

"Aw, hell," he growled in disgust. CeCe turned him on faster than any other woman he'd ever met. He decided the only solution was to stay as far away from her as possible. Before too long, her tempting, curvy body would be swollen with the child she carried. Surely that would cool the heat that raged inside him every time he got within touching distance.

Fortunately for CeCe's peace of mind, the moving van with her furniture and belongings arrived the next day. It took the two burly movers only an hour to unload her possessions.

CeCe waved goodbye and closed the door, leaning back against the wooden panels to survey the hall. Boxes were stacked against the wall all the way to the kitchen and back-bedroom doors; the stairway to the second floor had a box or two on each step, leaving only a narrow passage. She pushed away from the door and stepped around a box to reach the living room.

Boxes were stacked haphazardly on the floor and atop furniture. The padded, brown-paper-wrapped pieces of her dismantled weaving loom leaned against the far wall and she threaded her way between the boxes toward them.

"Hmm." She considered the size of the loom and scanned the room assessingly.

The southwest corner had windows that nearly met at the corner. She decided to take advantage of the sunlight available during the short winter days and began to shift boxes out of the corner, clearing floor space for the loom. She located the packing box holding her stereo system and took time out to unwrap it, plug it in and insert a compact disc.

She was happily shoving a large cardboard carton into the center of the room when the sound of a car engine broke into Glenn Miller's rendition of "String of Pearls." She turned down the volume on the stereo and peered out the living-room window. Jennifer Hightower was unbuckling her son, Steve, from a car seat, while Wayne and another young boy tossed snowballs at each other. A second woman, clearly in an advanced stage of pregnancy, stood waiting beside the car, holding a brown bag.

A smile lit CeCe's face. As promised, Jennifer Hightower had come to visit, and it appeared that she'd brought along a friend.

She hurriedly left the living room and pulled open the front door.

"Hello!" she called, waving at the two women.

"Hi, CeCe," Jennifer replied, propping her youngest on her hip. He squirmed to get down, but she tightened her grip, slammed the car door and started up the walk toward CeCe. "I brought my sister-in-law, Sarah, with me."

"Great." CeCe smiled at the two women and held the door wide. "Come on in, it's cold out there!"

"Oh, it's not cold," Jennifer laughingly admonished. "Not for Montana. Lucas says it's not really cold unless it's thirty below."

CeCe shivered and shook her head, eyeing Jennifer with trepidation as she retreated into the hall. "Is that normal? Thirty below zero?"

"Not really." Jennifer stepped across the threshold and swung Stevie to the floor, tugging him after her to the stairs. She let him climb to the second step before turning him to face her, then bent to untie his knit hat and unbutton his coat. "But Lucas keeps telling me that the weather has been mild during the years I've been here," she said over her shoulder as she stripped Stevie out of hat and coat. "There you go, sport." She took his hand and held him while he jumped down the steps to the hall floor. "CeCe, I'd like you to meet Sarah Drummond Hightower. She's married to my brother-in-law, Josh. Sarah, this is CeCe Hawkins."

"It's a pleasure to meet you." CeCe returned Sarah's smile with heartfelt warmth. Sarah slipped out of her long coat and CeCe realized that she was *very* pregnant.

"It's wonderful to have another woman in the neighborhood," Sarah replied as she handed CeCe a brown paper bag. "When Jennifer told me you'd moved in and she was coming to visit, I bribed her with cookies so that she'd bring me along.''

''Ah.'' CeCe took the bag and opened it, sniffing appreciatively as the aroma of fresh-baked cookies wafted out. ''My kind of women—you brought chocolate!''

The two women's laughter was interrupted by the abrupt opening of the front door.

''Mommy! Look at the cat!''

The two boys burst into the room, Wayne lugging Angus. The large orange-and-white cat was draped across Wayne's arm, a look of patient endurance on his features.

''Wow,'' Sarah breathed, her blue eyes widening. ''He's huge.''

''Yup. Really huge,'' Wayne agreed.

CeCe surmised the boy with Wayne must be Sarah's son. Beneath his bright red, wool knit cap, his hair was the same shade of silver-blond, and the twinkle in his green eyes was very like Sarah's.

''I bet Beastie and Rum would love him!'' the little boy continued.

''I bet Beastie and Rum would try to eat him, J.J.,'' Sarah said dryly. ''Dogs usually chase cats.''

''Nuh-uh!'' the two little boys protested loudly. ''Not Beastie and Rum—and this cat is really cool. What's his name, lady?''

CeCe was still struggling with the mental picture that leaped to mind at learning that Beastie and Rum were dogs. ''Uh, Angus,'' she said, collecting herself. ''His name is Angus.''

''How did he get so big?''

"I'm not sure," she said. "I've only had him a few years. He lived in an alley in Seattle near my office downtown. One day he followed me home and decided to stay. He's lived with me ever since."

"Wow," J.J. breathed. "So he's like a wild cat from the city! I bet he got in lots of fights. I bet that's where he got this humongous scar on his ear!"

CeCe nodded her head. The big cat had a three-cornered notch missing on one side of an ear. "I suspect you're probably right."

"I didn't know you moved here from Seattle!" Sarah exclaimed. "What a small world. Jennifer's from Seattle, too."

"I know. Come into the kitchen." CeCe gestured down the hallway. "If we can get there past all these boxes. I'll make another pot of coffee and you can tell me how you both came to live in this remote corner of Montana."

She led the way, weaving around stacked cardboard boxes, as the two women, three boys and one cat trailed after her.

"Have a seat," she invited. She emptied coffee grounds and refilled the coffeemaker. "So how *did* the two of you happen to land in Butte Creek?"

"Sarah was born here—her family's lived here for generations. I'm a schoolteacher," Jennifer explained. "I came here to substitute for a high-school teacher who couldn't complete the semester because she was having a difficult pregnancy."

"Unlike me," Sarah commented, smoothing her palm over the roundness of her belly. "I'm disgustingly healthy at the moment. I just keep getting fatter every day. I feel like a balloon that's about to pop.''

''When are you due?'' CeCe asked.

''The third week of December.'' Sarah heaved a sigh. ''I can hardly wait.''

''Mommy?'' J.J., who had stood patiently waiting while his mother answered CeCe's question, broke in. ''Can Wayne and I have a cookie?''

''Yes, J.J., you may, but take off your coat first.''

''Okay.''

The two boys quickly complied, took a cookie apiece from the bag and backed up against the kitchen cupboard, sliding downward until they sat, legs stretched out in front of them, on the linoleum floor.

''We must have caught you in the midst of unpacking,'' Jennifer said, plucking a cookie from the bag and breaking off a piece for Stevie. The little boy promptly tried to stuff it all in his mouth, beaming sunnily at CeCe.

''Actually, I just started.'' CeCe ripped the sealing tape off a box and pulled the flaps up, rummaging inside until she found some extra coffee mugs. ''The moving van was here this morning. It only took them about an hour to unload all my belongings, but I'm afraid it's going to take me a lot longer to unpack everything. I was just moving furniture and boxes in the living room to make an open space large enough to set up my loom when you arrived.''

Jennifer's face lit with interest. ''You have a loom?''

''Yes.'' CeCe filled the mugs and carried the coffee to the table.

"How fascinating," Sarah said. "Weaving is on my list of things to learn someday."

Jennifer rolled her eyes and laughed. "Her list is three pages long—but I have to confess that I've always been interested in weaving, too."

"Really?" CeCe was delighted. "I've been weaving since I was a child. I would sit and watch my grandmother for hours. When I was old enough, she let me help her on her loom. My dream has always been to find a way to weave full-time, and for the last five years I've marketed specialty items through several shops in Seattle."

"That's wonderful, CeCe. Will you continue now that you're in Montana?" Jennifer asked.

"Yes. I have commissions that I'm currently working on and the shop owners have assured me that they don't care where I live, just as long as I continue to produce."

"So you quit your day job, but kept the work you love?" Sarah commented. "You're so fortunate—that's every woman's dream."

"Yes, I guess it is," CeCe reflected, sipping her coffee. She smiled at the two women. "Would you like to see my grandmother's loom? I was just about to set it up."

"Yes," Jennifer said. "We'd love to, wouldn't we, Sarah?"

"Absolutely," Sarah responded. "Besides, maybe we could help. Unpacking is a real chore and we might as well be useful."

CeCe watched Sarah push herself up from the chair and was doubtful about just how much the very pregnant woman should be doing in her condition, but she didn't voice her concerns. Instead, she led the way into the living room and quickly shifted several small boxes off the sofa cushions.

"Have a seat, Sarah," she offered.

"Yes," Jennifer agreed. "Josh would have a fit if he knew you lifted anything heavier than your coffee cup."

"All right," Sarah conceded with a sigh. "I'll supervise while you two unpack."

"Deal," CeCe answered.

Jennifer pushed a packing box in front of the sofa and lifted Sarah's feet onto it. "There," she said. "Stay put."

"I thought I was the one who would be giving orders," Sarah protested.

"You are," Jennifer agreed with a grin. "But you have to put your feet up and rest while you're ordering us around. Otherwise, Josh will kill me for letting you run around and do too much."

"Hah," Sarah scoffed. "I can't run—I can only waddle."

CeCe smiled at the easy camaraderie between the two and smoothed a palm over the slight curve of her belly. "I can't wait until I'm waddling," she said wistfully.

Sarah and Jennifer went still, staring at her.

"Are you pregnant?" Sarah asked.

"Yes, nearly three and a half months," CeCe said, her voice a mixture of awe and delight. "The baby is due in mid-April."

"Congratulations," Jennifer said.

"Yes, congratulations." Sarah beamed at CeCe. "This is great—our babies will be born within a few months of each other. They can be playmates."

"Yes, they can." The warmth of Sarah and Jennifer's response to her news filled CeCe with pleasure. *This is going to work,* she told herself with a rush of relief. *Moving to Montana and building a new life was a good plan, with or without the complication of Zach Colby.*

At that very moment, Zach stomped out of the post office in Butte Creek, yanked open the door to his truck and climbed in. Moments later, he headed out of town toward the Hall ranch and CeCe Hawkins.

Muttering swearwords under his breath, he scowled out the windshield at the snowy landscape.

"Damn woman is probably lifting heavy boxes and shoving furniture around," he said to himself. The moment the postmistress told him that two men with a moving van had stopped to ask directions to the Hall ranch, he'd gotten an instant mental picture of CeCe hurting herself. "She's too stubborn to call and ask for help."

He'd watched Josh and Lucas fret, worry and scold Sarah and Jennifer the entire nine months their wives were pregnant. Because of them, he was well aware that a woman carrying a baby shouldn't lift anything heavier than a hairbrush. At least that was what Josh had told him—and Lucas had agreed.

He braked in front of CeCe's house and stepped out of the truck, his big Labrador, Cinders, trotting at his heels. He recognized Jennifer's sedan parked outside the gate, and by the time he strode up the steps and across the porch to knock on the door, he also recognized Jennifer's distinctive laugh followed by Sarah's voice.

"What is this?" he muttered. "A tea party?"

No one answered his knock. Instead, a fresh burst of feminine laughter reached him through the door panels, accompanied by children's giggles.

"Well, hell," he said in disgust, and opened the door. The laughter and chattering was coming from the living room. He crossed the hall and paused in the doorway, staring at the chaos in the cluttered room.

Sarah Hightower sat on the sofa, waving a feather duster at Jennifer and CeCe, her feet propped on a taped packing box. The two women stood in the far corner of the room, each holding one end of a wooden frame. Sarah gestured to the left and the two women shifted with the ungainly frame.

"Nope," Sarah said judiciously. "I think it ought to go just a bit to the right."

"Sarah," Jennifer said with exasperation. "Make up your mind! This thing is heavy!"

"Put that down."

The deep male voice startled them. The three women and three boys jumped in surprise, turning to stare at the man in the doorway.

Zach stalked across the room and with one hand took the wooden frame from CeCe's grasp. He slid his other arm around her waist and lifted her out of the way with easy strength before he and Jennifer rested the frame against the wall. He turned, hands

on hips, and fixed the speechless CeCe with a narrow, threatening stare.

"You," he said with deadly emphasis, "shouldn't be lifting anything heavier than a coffee cup." His gaze shifted to fasten with equal laserlike intensity on the openmouthed Sarah. "And neither should you."

Ignoring the wide-eyed stares from Jennifer and Sarah, he stripped off his jacket and picked up a box.

"I'll move boxes and anything else you want moved," he said firmly. "You confine yourself to giving directions. Where do you want this?"

CeCe glared at him. He glared back, his chin set stubbornly.

"Is this part of your 'I feel responsible' syndrome?" she demanded.

"No," he said shortly. "This is just being neighborly."

"Hmmph," CeCe snorted inelegantly. She badly wanted to tell him to drop the box and get out of her house and out of her life. Unfortunately, he was much bigger, much stronger and much more capable of moving heavy boxes. Besides, she thought reluctantly, she really didn't want to chance harming the baby, no matter how remote the possibility. "In that case," she said with a conscious effort at graciousness, "I thank you."

"You're welcome," Zach said gruffly. "Where do you want this box?"

"In the kitchen."

Zach nodded abruptly and turned away. He paused in front of Sarah.

"Will you phone Josh? He's at my place working

on the baler. Ask him to come over and bring Charlie—and Murphy, if he's still around—to help move boxes and furniture.''

"Sure, Zach.'' He was already moving away when Sarah managed to push herself up from the sofa. She rolled her eyes at Jennifer and CeCe. "Men! They can be so bossy, can't they?''

CeCe couldn't help it, her irritation with Zach dissolved and she burst into laughter.

"Meow!''

A bundle of orange-and-white fur leaped from a chair back and landed heavily on CeCe's shoulder.

"Hey!'' She reached up and pried the cat loose. "What are you…''

The cat growled, the hair on his back lifting. His ears flattened against his head, his gold eyes glowing.

"No, no, Cinders!'' J.J. caught the heavy red collar encircling a huge black Labrador's thick neck and pulled. "You're not allowed to eat the cat—you have to be friends!''

CeCe stared in astonishment at the big dog. He was clearly a purebred, and judging from the size of his feet he wasn't done growing yet, even though his head was almost level with her waist. His velvety brown eyes were alert, his ears lifted with interest and his tail wagged with friendly curiosity.

"Cinders, down.''

The dog's head swung around at the deep-voiced command, his tail wagging even faster, but he sat obediently.

"Sorry about that.'' Zach plucked Angus from CeCe's arms and deposited him on the top shelf of an empty bookcase shoved against the wall. "Cinders wouldn't hurt the cat. We have a dozen barn cats at home and they're all on friendly terms. He's just curious."

"Oh," CeCe said faintly, eyeing the large dog. "He's certainly big."

"That's the understatement of the year," Jennifer said dryly. "He's almost as tall as Beastie, my dog and Cinders's father."

"Jennifer and her two dogs are the reason for an explosion in the dog population of Daniels County," Zach commented, a swift grin breaking across his features as Jennifer made a face at him. "She brought a giant brown Labrador named Beastie with her from Seattle, and then Lucas gave her Cinderella, a yellow female. Every time those two have a litter of pups, Jennifer strong-arms her friends and neighbors into adopting the little ones. That's how I got CinderFella last year."

"CinderFella? Cinderella? Beastie?" CeCe repeated the names. "Did you name them after characters in Disney films?"

"Nope," Jennifer denied. "I gave them all names from fairy tales."

"Yeah," J.J. interjected. "My daddy's dog is named Rumpelstiltskin—but it's a really long name, so we just call him Rum."

"Oh, I see." CeCe nodded, bemused. Cinders chose that moment to stretch toward her and nudge her fingers with his wet nose. CeCe turned her hand over and let him sniff. He responded by licking her palm with his pink, wet tongue.

CeCe laughed and bent forward to rub the huge dog between the ears.

Zach's breath caught. Her throaty chuckle was powerfully seductive and he tamped down the urge to toss her over his shoulder and head for the nearest bed.

She's pregnant, he reminded himself grimly. *She was married to Aaron. She's off limits.* Zach's fingers curled into fists and he jammed his hands into his pockets to keep from reaching for her.

She glanced up at him, laughing, and her fingers stilled in Cinders's fur, her expression swiftly changing to wary watchfulness.

"What box do you want moved next?" he asked gruffly, glancing away from her and around the room.

CeCe straightened. He'd knocked her off balance, again. She glanced across the room and chose a box at random.

"If you'd move the big carton labeled Dishes into the kitchen, I can unpack and empty that box while you're working in here."

"All right." Zach nodded abruptly and strode across the room to shoulder the carton.

Jennifer swept up Stevie. "We'll help you in the kitchen, CeCe. Sarah can sit at the table and unwrap dishes and I'll help put them away."

"First I have to phone Josh," Sarah said.

"The phone's in the kitchen," CeCe said. "It's a cell phone on the cabinet next to the refrigerator."

The three women retraced their way into the kitchen, skirting boxes and furniture on the way. Zach was just exiting the kitchen and stood aside to let them pass.

"What do you want moved next?" he asked CeCe.

She stopped and looked back down the hall. "The boxes are all marked on the tops and sides with the room where they need to be unpacked. If you could move them into the right rooms, then I can manage unpacking."

Zach surveyed the crowded hall. "That takes care of the living room, kitchen and bathroom. Which bedroom are you using?"

"The bedroom on the ground floor."

Zach's gaze swept over her, and CeCe's face heated beneath his swift glance.

"Right." He took a step down the hall before he halted and looked back at her. "Did Sarah call Josh?"

"She's going to now," CeCe confirmed.

"Good."

He strode down the hall and disappeared into the living room.

CeCe was on her third carton of china and glassware, standing ankle deep in a sea of discarded packing paper, when she heard the muffled growl of vehicle engines outside.

"Daddy's here!" Wayne shouted.

Wayne and J.J., followed by Stevie and Cinders, raced out of the kitchen. CeCe heard the clatter of their boots down the hallway, followed by the distinctive low squeak of the front door.

"Hi, Daddy!"

"Hey, Slugger."

CeCe recognized Lucas's deep voice, followed by several other male voices as they greeted the boys and Zach. The tramp of heavy boots sounded down the hall, nearing the kitchen. She slid a stack of china plates onto the second shelf of the kitchen cabinet and glanced over her shoulder just as four men, three boys and two huge Labrador dogs moved through the doorway and crowded into the kitchen.

Lucas bent and dropped a kiss on Jennifer's mouth. A tall, broad-shouldered man who could only be his brother did the same to Sarah. Behind the two, Charlie touched the brim of his hat and smiled a greeting at CeCe. The old-fashioned kitchen seemed to shrink, crowded as it was.

"CeCe." Sarah claimed her attention. "This is my husband, Josh."

"Hello." CeCe smiled in greeting. Josh's black hair, handsome face and startling turquoise eyes bore a striking resemblance to Lucas's.

"It's a pleasure to meet you." Josh glanced around the kitchen, a grin growing. "Looks like you've got more help than you can stand."

CeCe laughed and surveyed the kitchen. Empty boxes were stacked haphazardly atop each other in one corner; Sarah had unpacked the contents of two smaller boxes onto the table, and the surface was buried beneath glasses, coffee mugs and a stack of napkins, towels and place mats. "It's a little crowded at the moment," she admitted. "But I'm delighted to have so much help."

Lucas smiled at her and looked at Zach. "What do you want us to do?"

Zach pushed away from the doorjamb, where he'd been leaning, and uncrossed his arms. "I've been moving boxes into the rooms where they belong while the women unpack. When we finish that, we can put beds together and there's a wooden contraption that needs assembling."

"That *wooden contraption* is my grandmother's antique loom," CeCe interjected.

Zach flicked her a glance. "There's a loom to put together," he continued as if she hadn't spoken. "And I assume most of the Halls' furniture will have to be moved into storage."

"Oh, that's right," CeCe said worriedly. "Where can we put it?"

"Is there an attic?" Jennifer asked.

"I don't know." CeCe tucked a strand of hair behind one ear. Her fingertips, stained with newsprint from the papers used to cushion the packed glass, left a black smudge across the high arch of her cheek.

"If there isn't, we can store stuff in one of the outbuildings," Zach reassured her. *She looks tired.* "Did you take a nap today?" he asked abruptly, frowning at her.

"No," she said shortly, frowning back at him. "But I slept late this morning."

Zach continued to assess her for a long moment, ignoring her irritated, challenging glare.

"All right," he said. "But if you get tired, go to bed. We can finish moving stuff today and come back to unpack the boxes tomorrow."

CeCe's eyes narrowed and a sharp retort hovered on the tip of her tongue. She glanced away from him in an attempt to rein in her temper and realized that the other five adults in the room were watching her and Zach with expressions that held a mix of disbelief, astonishment and curiosity. The fascinated audience effectively dampened her rising temper.

"Of course," she said sweetly through her teeth. "Whatever you say, Mr. Colby."

Zach's eyebrows winged upward in surprise. She was agreeing? With no argument? Beside him, Lucas shifted and Zach glanced sideways, catching his friend's amused expression. A swift scan of the other adults in the room told him exactly why the widow was being cooperative.

"We'll start in the hallway," he said abruptly.

He turned on his heel and left the room, followed by the other three men, the boys and the dogs.

"Well," CeCe said brightly, ignoring the significant look Jennifer and Sarah exchanged. "I'll get some of this paper off the floor and we can open another box." She bent and swept up an armful of crinkled newspaper and crossed the room to stuff it into an empty box.

Behind her, Jennifer ripped the sealing tape from another carton and set it atop a chair seat in front of Sarah. "You unpack this one, Sarah, while I move the glasses off the tabletop to the counter," she said. "Where should I put the linens, CeCe?"

Relieved that the two women weren't going to question Zach's comments, CeCe uttered a silent thank-you and turned to face them.

move the furniture that's in there upstairs into one of the empty rooms and have my own bed and dresser set up down here, if it's not too much trouble.''

''Nope, not at all.'' Zach wished she'd stop looking at him like that. He was having enough trouble trying to ignore the vivid mental images that crowded his mind after he'd unearthed the four-poster brass bed leaning against the wall in the living room. He didn't need to see her gray eyes widen and turn smoky to imagine in painful detail just how she'd look lying in that big bed. Preferably naked. Preferably with both of them naked. Preferably with her soft, silky body pinned under his. He clenched his teeth, nodded curtly and got the hell out of the kitchen.

CeCe and Zach spent the remainder of the afternoon carefully avoiding each other. If Jennifer and Sarah noticed, they didn't comment. The short winter day fled before an early dusk, and Jennifer and Sarah gathered their children, pried their husbands away from the football game on the television set the men had hooked up in the living room and herded them all toward waiting cars and trucks. Zach said his goodbyes and left, too.

Wrapped in a soft blue, woven, knee-length shawl, CeCe stood in the doorway and waved goodbye, calling promises that she'd visit them soon. She was tired, but pleased that they'd done so much work. It would have taken her days to accomplish so much alone.

She closed the door and walked down the hall, pausing in the doorway to her bedroom. The big brass bed stood against the far wall, lamps glowing gently on top of the two bedside tables. The pillows were plumped against the headboard, the sheets turned back over the soft rose-colored comforter and hand-woven cream throw. The tops of the antique cherry-wood dresser and matching dressing table gleamed with fresh polish.

The room was warmly inviting and a wave of weariness washed over her.

"Maybe I'll take a short nap," she murmured to herself. A warm, furry body brushed against her ankles and she glanced down.

"Hello, Angus. Where have you been hiding? Didn't you like those big dogs?" She bent and picked him up, brushing her chin against the top of his head and the tufted tips of his ears. "Don't worry. You'll get used to them."

The throaty growl sounded suspiciously like a snort of disbelief, but CeCe ignored him. She carried him into the room and set him down atop the coverlet at the end of the bed. "Take a nap with me, Angus. We've both had a long, exhausting day."

Angus padded in a circle, kneaded the soft woven throw with his claws and settled down, curling into a ball.

CeCe gave him a last pat, shrugged the warm shawl off her shoulders and dropped it across the seat of the old rocker near the window before slipping out of her jeans and sweater and climbing into bed. She was asleep almost as soon as her head hit the pillow.

Two days passed before Zach returned to the Hall ranch. He had a list of things that needed to be checked on at the ranch, and the first was to inspect the tractors, trucks and other equipment. Like most ranchers, he spent the short winter days doing maintenance and necessary repair work in preparation for the busy spring and summer.

The midmorning sun glittered off the snow when he pulled his truck into the farm lot and parked in front of the machine shop. He stepped out of the pickup and glanced at the house. It was ten o'clock in the morning and CeCe was probably awake, but nothing stirred at the house.

I'll look at the machinery before I go up to the house to check the roof and weather stripping, he decided.

He bypassed the wide, roll-back garage doors that took up nearly the entire front wall of the building and entered through a small door at the far left. The inside of the metal building was gloomy and he flipped the light switch. Bright electric shop fixtures, mounted near the high, two-story ceiling, flooded the cavernous room with light. The dark, shadowy shapes of machinery became tractors, a combine, a baler, and near the front door, CeCe's small car.

The huge room was freezing and Zach turned up the thermostat. The furnace rattled and banged as it came to life; he knew it would take time to warm the vast space and he left his coat on as he moved methodically from machine to machine. His mood worsened with each piece of equipment he inspected.

"Damn." He finished his circuit of the room and halted near the door, eyes narrowed in disgust as he surveyed the room. From the condition of the equipment, it was clear that in the time Aaron Hall had operated the ranch, he had spent little effort or money maintaining and repairing the expensive machinery that crammed the shop.

Zach snapped off the light, left the thermostat on low and stepped outside. He squinted against the bright glare of sunlight off brilliant white snow as he headed toward the house.

I hope the house is in better shape, he thought grimly. *If not, the widow must have spent a few uncomfortable nights.*

CeCe heard the knock on her front door and left her loom. She knew it was Zach. She'd watched him park his truck in front of the machine shop and disappear inside. After several minutes, when the lights went on and he didn't come out, she'd gone back to her work on the loom.

She braced herself and pulled open the door. The shock of electrical awareness that raced through her veins at the sight of his tall, broad figure was becoming all too familiar. He wore boots and jeans under his sheepskin-lined coat and the brim of his black Stetson shaded his eyes from the snow glare.

"Good morning, Zach."

"Morning." Zach touched the brim of his hat in brief greeting. "I stopped by to take a look at the roof and the weather stripping around the windows and doors."

"Of course." CeCe opened the door wide. "Come in."

Zach stamped the snow off his boots and stepped across the threshold, removing his hat. The house was blessedly warm and the scents of baking and freshly brewed coffee hung on the air.

"Have you had any trouble keeping the house warm enough to be comfortable?" he asked, unbuttoning his coat.

"No." CeCe shook her head. "Should I?"

"I don't know," he answered. "But given the condition of the machinery in the shop, I wouldn't be surprised if the house needs maintenance work. Are any windows or doors rattling or leaking cold air around the sills?"

"I haven't noticed any cold drafts." CeCe frowned and glanced up the stairway. "But I have heard what sounds like a loose window making noise upstairs when the wind blows from the north. I checked the bedrooms but didn't find anything. All the windows seemed to be latched and secure."

"I'll see if I can find what's causing the noise when I go upstairs," Zach said. "But I'll start on this floor first and make sure the doors and windows are tight." He glanced sideways to find CeCe eyeing him with exasperation. "If that's all right with you," he added, belatedly remembering his manners.

A wry smile tilted the corners of her full mouth and amusement lit the depths of her gray eyes.

"Are you asking?"

He tried to ignore the lure of dancing eyes and the sweet, upward curve of her mouth. "Yeah," he growled reluctantly. "I'm asking."

"Then it's all right with me," CeCe said promptly, her smile widening at his scowl. "I know it's difficult for you to ask instead of ordering, so I appreciate your consideration.''

"Yeah," he muttered, unwilling to let her see his response to her teasing. His hormones were saner when she was frowning at him. "Right." He glanced around and shifted uncomfortably. "Well…"

"Why don't you let me take your coat and hat," CeCe suggested, holding out her hand. "It's much too warm in here for that heavy jacket."

Zach handed her his hat and shrugged out of the coat. She took it and walked into the living room, folding the jacket over the back of a chair and setting the hat on the seat.

"Is there anything I can do to help?" she asked, turning to him.

"No," he responded.

"Then I'll go back to work and stay out of your way." CeCe was determined to keep her encounters with Zach on a neutral, friendly footing. Just because the mere sight of him knocked her heart sideways and sent her blood pressure skyrocketing didn't mean that she had to let him know how he affected her, nor that she had to act on what she considered a completely inappropriate attraction. Because of her baby, theirs was going to be a long-term, platonic relationship. She needed to reach a comfort zone. Just how she was going to do that, she had no idea.

She sat down at the loom and tried to concentrate on the pattern she was developing. Her heightened senses, however, were constantly aware of Zach's progress around the room as he efficiently checked the weather stripping and the fit of the windows.

He left the room and she heaved a sigh of relief. She could hear him moving through the kitchen and bathroom and knew the moment he reached her bedroom.

The sound of his boots abruptly ceased.

What's he doing? She tried to remember if she'd left any lingerie lying on top of the dresser or bed. She'd been unpacking boxes earlier and tucking underwear and nighties into drawers in the 1940s vanity.

The sound of his boots resumed and CeCe drew a deep breath, only then realizing that she'd been sitting frozen, hardly breathing.

She heard him stride back down the hall and bent her head, pretending to be engrossed in her weaving. He didn't pause at the living-room door, but continued up the stairs. Her fingers moved automatically back and forth, her senses tuned to his movements upstairs. At last, she heard him descend the stairs and she glanced up. He paused in the doorway.

"You're right. One of the windows in the back bedroom upstairs is loose. I've got tools and weather stripping in the truck. It won't take long to fix it."

"Is that the only window that needs to be fixed?"

"As far as I can tell," Zach said. "I'm surprised— the house is in better shape than the outbuildings."

"Is there a lot of work to be done on them?" CeCe had a sudden picture of the barn, shed, shop and the other outbuildings listing or collapsing beneath the snow.

"Enough," Zach said with disgust. "But repair and maintenance on the farm machinery will take the most time. We're lucky this is winter and not spring planting season. I should have plenty of time to fix everything.''

''Planting season? What crops do you grow here?'' CeCe asked, her curiosity piqued.

''I'm not sure what I'll plant *here*,'' Zach replied, ''but on my own place, I seed mostly wheat, barley and oats.''

''Oh.'' CeCe tried to remember what Jennifer and Sarah had told her about the Hightower ranches. ''I thought Sarah told me that you and her husband were partners in a quarterhorse-breeding operation?''

''We are,'' Zach agreed. ''But all three of our ranches are diversified. We have pasture for the horses and cattle, plus acres seeded in grain crops.''

''Do you raise hay for the horses and cattle?''

''No, not much,'' Zach answered. ''This part of Montana is dryland farming. Alfalfa is the best hay for cattle and horses, but to grow alfalfa you need plenty of water to irrigate, which we can't do in this county. We buy alfalfa from western Montana to feed the stock through the winter. We do bale a little grass hay here, but that's about all, and Josh and I raise enough oats to grain the horses.''

CeCe was fascinated. ''This is all so very different from my life in Seattle.'' She glanced out the window and across the wide, snowy lot to the big barn. ''Will you be using this barn to keep horses? Or cattle?''

Zach shrugged. ''I hadn't thought much about it, but I suppose we might.''

CeCe's eyes glowed with anticipation and delight. ''I hope you do. It would be such fun to have animals here. Could we have chickens? And barn cats? Maybe a dog?''

He gave her a quizzical look. "I wasn't considering anything but horses and cattle, but I reckon you can have any of those things you want. If you get chickens, you'll have to take care of them yourself—and I've gotta tell you, chickens are about the stupidest critters God ever made.''

CeCe frowned at him. "But baby chicks are such cute little balls of yellow fuzz.''

Zach rolled his eyes. "Lady, it's easy to see you've never lived on a farm. Those cute little fuzzy yellow chicks grow up to be hens that peck holes in your hand when you try to collect their eggs, or roosters that attack if you turn your back.''

"I don't believe you," she protested. "You're just saying that because you know very well I know nothing at all about chickens.''

"Trust me, I'm not lying," he said with conviction. "When I was a kid, my grandfather had a big white rooster that attacked everything that went near the barn—especially me, every time I turned my back on the wily bird.''

"What did you do to antagonize him?'' CeCe asked suspiciously, unwilling to completely abandon her romantic picture of a peaceful, motherly clutch of hens protected by a strutting, fatherly rooster.

"Nothing, I swear.'' Zach raised his right hand. "That rooster was just plain hostile.''

"Hmm.'' CeCe reluctantly accepted that perhaps he was telling the truth. "What about cats and dogs? Do you have any objections to them?''

"Nope, not a one."

"How about sheep?" she asked.

"No sheep," he retorted. "No way."

"Why not?"

"Because I raise horses and cattle. No sheep."

"But I've always wanted to raise my own sheep, shear their wool and weave the thread on my loom. Having control of the entire process from the beginning to the end product is a dream of mine."

Zach eyed her with a mix of exasperation and disgust. "I'm a cattleman," he said firmly. "I do *not* raise sheep."

CeCe glared at him. His jaw was set with stubbornness. His deep voice held a note of finality. "We'll see," she said, refusing to concede.

"I'll get my tools out of the truck and fix the window upstairs," he told her, obviously through with the subject.

"All right," she murmured. *We'll see who wins this battle,* she thought as he left the house.

Her grandmother had raised sheep on her small Bainbridge Island acreage across the Puget Sound from Seattle, and CeCe had loved to visit her and tend the gentle creatures. She'd also loved the wonderful wool they gave up each year for her grandmother to dye, spin into yarn and use to create the distinctive patterns on the old loom.

CeCe wanted to re-create those memories for her own child. Come hell or high water, in spite of the stubborn rancher's obvious dislike of sheep, that was just what she was going to do.

* * *

"Hey, Zach! Hold up."

Zach paused, his hand on the open truck door, and looked over his shoulder. Charlie limped toward him across the snowy lot from the barn.

"Damned arthritis," he complained good-naturedly. "These cold mornings play hob with my knees."

"Yeah," Zach said with sympathy. "I have to admit I'm a little slow about rollin' out of bed myself on mornings when the thermometer barely reaches zero."

"The older you get, the worse it is. It's hell gettin' old, boy," Charlie warned him. "Don't do it."

Zach grinned. "I'm not sure I like the only alternative, Charlie."

Charlie chuckled, his blue eyes twinkling beneath shaggy eyebrows. "I hear you. I guess there's nothing to do but put up with the aches."

"Yeah, I think you're right," Zach agreed.

"Of course, if a man were smart," Charlie said sagely, his bright gaze fixed on Zach's face, "he'd find himself a nice, sweet woman to keep him warm on cold winter nights."

"Hah," Zach grunted in easy derision. "You're a fine one to talk. You've been a bachelor for more than sixty years."

"True," the older man agreed, "but just because I never found a good woman to marry don't mean I'm too dumb to know that I'd be a lot warmer if I had a woman to cuddle in bed."

"Maybe," Zach said noncommittally. "Did you holler at me just to discuss how cold the weather is?"

"Nope," Charlie answered promptly. "I wanted to ask you if you're on your way into town."

"No, I'm going over to the Hall place to take apart the tractor engine. Why? Did you need something from town?"

"Yeah. Thought I might save me a trip if you were goin', but since you're not, I reckon I'll run on in to the feed store myself." Charlie paused. "You plannin' on sayin' hello to Ms. Hawkins while you're over at the Hall place?"

"Nope." Zach ignored the older man's speculative gaze and stepped into the truck. "When Josh shows up, tell him I'll be gone most of the day."

"Sure thing." Charlie waited until the pickup door was almost closed. "Tell Ms. Hawkins hello for me."

Zach scowled, but Charlie grinned and turned away, limping back toward the warmth of the big old barn.

"Hell," Zach muttered, turning the key with an irritated twist. "What makes him think I'm going over there to see CeCe? I told him I've got two months' worth of work on that damn machinery."

CeCe heard Zach's truck and watched him park outside the machine shop. This was the fourth day in a row he'd arrived at nine in the morning. The first day she'd been on edge, expecting him to knock on her door, but he'd spent the day inside the shop and had left just before dusk. The second and third days had been repeats of the first.

She was struggling with adapting to the quiet, solitary life in the country after her busy, noisy days in

Seattle. Zach's arrival was a break in the long, peaceful hours and she found herself listening for the sound of his truck each morning.

"Oh, for Pete's sake," she muttered, snapping the curtain back in place. "I must be really desperate for the sound of a human voice if I'm actually looking forward to arguing with Zach."

"Meow?"

CeCe glanced over her shoulder and found Angus watching her, curled comfortably atop the back of the sofa. He blinked at her, his whiskers twitching in disbelief.

She crossed the room and scooped him up, cuddling him and rubbing him under the chin as she walked into the kitchen.

"You're such a critic," she chided him. "And you never believe anything I say." She set him down on the rug in front of the sink and pulled open the upper cabinet where she kept the coffee. He chirped at her and she glanced down at him. "All right," she conceded. "I admit he makes my heart go crazy, but I refuse to let him know."

The big cat, nose in the air and tail stiffly erect, turned his back on her and stalked out of the room.

CeCe shrugged. "Traitor." She called after him, "You males are all the same. Impossible."

There was no answering yowl from the living room. CeCe shook her head.

"CeCe Hawkins," she said aloud, "you're losing it. Not only are you talking to a cat, but you're actually expecting him to answer you."

She filled the coffeemaker with water and measured

coffee into the filter, leaning against the counter and gazing out at the snowy buttes while she waited. The brewing light clicked off and she filled a mug, then turned to leave the room. Her glance fell on the borrowed cellular phone on the end of the counter. Just above it hung the wall phone the installer had connected three days ago.

She eyed the small phone for a long moment.

Should she walk out to the shop and return it to Zach with her thanks?

Of course she should. She'd planned to give it to Charlie the next time he plowed the snow from her lane, but returning the phone to Zach in person was both practical and polite.

Of course she shouldn't. Hadn't she decided to avoid the rancher unless absolutely necessary?

"Should I, or shouldn't I?"

The house was silent. Not even Angus rumbled in response from the living room.

If she wanted to hear a human voice other than her own, she could pick up the phone and call Jennifer or Sarah. Or get in the car and drive into town to the cafe.

But Zach was within walking distance. And she did need to return the phone.

With sudden decisiveness, she took another mug from the cabinet and filled it. She caught up her jacket from the back of a chair and shrugged into it, wrapping a wool muffler around her neck. She tucked the phone into her coat pocket and picked up the two steaming mugs.

She juggled the two mugs on her way out the front

door and as she struggled to open the door to the machine shop. Cinders met her inside, his tail wagging, his damp nose bumping her jeans-clad knee in greeting.

"Hi, fella." She smiled down at him. He panted happily up at her, his brown eyes alight with friendly interest. "Where's your owner?"

"Who's there?"

Zach's voice was muffled. CeCe searched the room and finally located him beside a huge piece of machinery. Bent over an engine, he had his back to her.

"Is that you, Charlie?"

"No," CeCe replied. "It's me."

Zach twisted around and looked over his shoulder. She stood near the door, a steaming mug in each hand. Her cheeks were pink with cold, a red wool scarf tucked around her throat and under her chin, her dark hair falling loosely to her shoulders.

CeCe shifted uneasily. He didn't say a word, just looked at her. "I brought you some coffee." She lifted one of the cups and his gaze flicked from her face to the mug, then back up to meet her eyes. "I thought you might want something hot to drink."

He still didn't answer and she frowned at him in irritation. "What? You're not speaking to me today?"

His mouth lifted in a swift grin, his tense figure visibly loosening. He picked up a rag and turned to face her, wiping black grease from his hands as he leaned back against the tractor cab.

"Sure, I'm speaking. I'm just surprised to see you, that's all."

"I don't know why," she said testily, skirting the

front bumper of her car as she walked toward him. "I live here, after all."

"True." Zach searched her face as he took the mug from her outstretched hand and lifted it to his lips. He sipped, swallowed and wondered what she was really doing here. "Good coffee," he commented. "Thanks."

"You're welcome." CeCe sipped her own coffee and glanced around her at the interior of the shop. "Does all of this machinery need work?"

"Most of it." Zach nodded at the tractor he leaned against and the greasy engine parts laid out on the concrete floor. "The engine on this old tractor is the worst, but nearly everything in here needs repairs of one kind or another."

She surveyed the room again. "It looks like an enormous task for one man. Will you be able to finish everything before spring?"

"Probably." Zach shrugged. "If not, Charlie or Murphy will help. They're both pretty good mechanics."

"Are they relatives?" CeCe asked curiously, not certain where the two older men fit in the picture she was slowly forming of Butte Creek.

"No, we're not blood relations," Zach replied. "They own a ranch south of the Hightower spread, but a fire burned the house down years ago. They're both bachelors and they went to live with a neighbor, Wayne Scanlon, while they rebuilt the barn. Wayne was a bachelor, too, and back then, Lucas and Josh were just two high-school kids who lived with him after their mom left and their dad died. To make a long story short, Charlie and Murphy never did get around to rebuilding the house. They stayed on with Wayne, and after he died they simply stayed with Lucas and Josh. They farm the acres and run cattle on their own place, but they live on the Hightower spread.''

"And you and Josh Hightower are in business together, so Charlie and Murphy work with you, too?''

"Something like that.'' Zach eyed her. Concentration drew two little lines between her dark eyebrows. "You look confused.''

CeCe glanced quickly up from her coffee mug. "No, not confused, exactly. It's just that I've never known men who willingly worked for free.''

"It's not for free, exactly,'' Zach corrected her. "If they need my help, all they have to do is ask.''

"In my experience,'' she said dryly, "asking for help with a job only got me a variety of excuses why my friends would love to help but just couldn't. Except for relatives, of course. My parents and sister were always supportive, but they love me. Relatives usually feel they're stuck with helping. But you're not even related to Charlie and Murphy.''

"No, thank God,'' he said shortly. "The only relatives I've ever liked were my grandfather and my mother.''

Belatedly, CeCe remembered that Zach's relationship with his biological father was not a subject he would likely want to discuss. But her curiosity drove her to ask about his other family. "Do your mother and grandfather live in Butte Creek?''

"They used to. My mother married and moved to

Missoula ten years ago, soon after my grandfather passed away.''

"I'm sorry." So he had lost both his beloved mother and grandfather at nearly the same time. "Was he ill very long?"

"No," he replied. "Granddad went to sleep one night in the middle of summer, and sometime before morning he had a massive heart attack. The doctor said he died instantly—probably never even knew what hit him."

"Oh." She tried to imagine what it must have been like to lose a loved one so swiftly. Her own grandfather had passed away when she was a young child and she could barely remember him. Her beloved grandmother had had a heart condition that kept her family constantly concerned, but the knowledge that she had a weak heart had given them years of preparation. Still, they'd grieved. "I'm sorry. I lost my grandmother a year ago. I still miss her."

The quiet, genuine emotion in her voice was reflected in her soft gray eyes. Zach was startled and uncomfortable with the alien and unsettling sense that this woman saw into his heart and understood his loss. He'd never known that feeling with another human, not even his mother, Josh or Lucas.

"It gets a little easier after a few more years," he offered gruffly.

"Do you ever stop missing them?"

"No. But you smile more often."

"Ah," she said, understanding.

Silence reigned for a few moments, each of them lost in their own thoughts. Cinders broke the stillness when he barked loudly and raced across the room to the far corner.

CeCe jumped, clutching her mug. "What is it? What's wrong?"

"Nothing," Zach reassured her. "There's a family of field mice living in that back corner. Every now and then Cinders feels the need to let them know that he's around."

"Will he kill them?"

"Nah, I doubt it." Zach laughed. "The likelihood that he can catch one of them is zero to none. Those little guys are fast."

"You sound like you hope he doesn't catch them."

"I do." He grinned at her. "Now, if there were grain stored in this building, I'd borrow that cat of yours to hunt them. But there isn't anything in here that they can hurt."

"So you believe in live and let live?"

"Sure—as long as they don't eat anything that belongs to me."

CeCe burst into laughter. "If that doesn't sound like a man," she teased. "Why are men so territorial?"

"You think women aren't?" he questioned lazily.

"Not nearly as much as men," she answered promptly.

"Hah. Women are every bit as protective of what they've staked out as their territory. Believe me, I know from experience. Sarah Hightower chased me out of her kitchen with a flyswatter once."

"What did you do?" CeCe asked suspiciously.

"Nothing much." Zach's eyes twinkled. "All I did

was walk across her kitchen floor and take a handful of cookies.''

CeCe was sure that wasn't the whole story. ''And?'' she prompted.

''And what?''

''And why did she chase you out? There must be more you're not telling me.''

''Well...'' Zach's eyes narrowed consideringly. ''I guess I did forget to mention that it was pouring rain outside, my boots were muddy, and she'd just scrubbed and waxed the floor.''

''Well, no wonder she chased you!'' CeCe shook her head at him in disgust. ''You're lucky all she was carrying was a flyswatter. Had it been me, I'd have sicced Angus on you while I looked for my gun.''

''You have a gun?''

''Well, no,'' CeCe admitted. ''But maybe I should get one.''

''No,'' he answered abruptly. ''You don't need a gun. Besides, I've learned my lesson. If it's raining, I always take my boots off and leave them at the door. Sarah refused to bake cookies for me for two months after I got her floor dirty.''

''I take it you like cookies?''

''Yup.'' He nodded. ''Josh and I are both push-overs for double chocolate chip with pecans.''

CeCe laughed. ''I'll have to remember that if I ever need to bribe you, I should offer you cookies.''

No, offer yourself. The swift, unbidden thought caught Zach off guard and he realized that he'd been chatting with CeCe as easily as if they were old friends. *Don't forget who she is,* he told himself.

He tilted the mug and drained the remaining coffee, handing the empty cup back to her.

"Thanks for the coffee," he told her. "I'd better get back to work if I plan to get this engine back together before spring."

CeCe recognized the dismissal in his tone.

"And I need to get back to the house." She turned and was halfway to the door before she remembered the phone in her pocket. "Oh, I nearly forgot." She retraced her steps and held out the phone. "The phone company installed my phone a few days ago—thanks so much for letting me borrow this."

"You're welcome." Zach took the small phone and tucked it into his shirt pocket.

CeCe nodded and turned away again. She pulled open the door and looked over her shoulder at him. "Do you realize we've actually had a normal conversation?" she commented. "We didn't argue once."

"Amazing," Zach said dryly.

"Maybe we should practice," she said consideringly. "I'll bring you coffee again tomorrow. Perhaps if we really concentrate, we can slowly work our way up to an entire half hour of conversation without an argument."

"I don't know—a half hour might be pushing it."

She shrugged. "Everyone's got to have a goal. Thirty minutes is a nice round number. Besides, any discussions we need to have about the baby probably won't take more than a half hour."

"Yeah." Zach wished she wouldn't look so damn

cute at the same time she was talking about the baby. *Aaron's baby.* He had to remember that she probably wouldn't be making the effort to talk to him at all if it wasn't for Kenneth Hall's last will and testament.

Chapter Five

"Maybe we should think about it," CeCe said hastily. She wondered what Zach was thinking. He wore an inscrutable expression that was becoming all too familiar. Suddenly, her impulsive offer to share coffee and conversation seemed more dangerous than wise. "I'd hate to have us rush into anything." She bent and patted Cinders on the head. "Bye, Cinders—don't eat the mice."

And she whisked quickly out the door.

Zach stood motionless, staring at the closed door. He ought to be glad she was reconsidering sharing morning coffee with him. The less contact he had with CeCe the better. She was too pretty for comfort and when she wasn't arguing with him, she had a way of slipping under his guard and making him laugh. Beauty and humor were a lethal combination. Not to mention the fact that he couldn't remember talking this much in years.

He rarely wasted time talking with women—at least, not conversations that lasted very long. It didn't take a lot of words to ask the divorcée in the next county if she was in the mood for sex, nor did they spend a lot of time chatting after they were done. He spent little time in the company of women, with the exception of Jennifer and Sarah. And if they hadn't married his best friends, he doubted that he would have more than a passing acquaintance with them.

And that would have been a shame, he mused, because he thought the world of both of them. No one who knew Josh and Lucas could doubt the genuine joy their wives and children had brought to their lives.

Of course, he reflected grimly, *neither of them had been married to Aaron Hall and pregnant with his baby.*

He scrubbed his hand over his face and turned back to the stubborn engine, determined to put CeCe Hawkins out of his mind.

CeCe was having second thoughts of her own. The following day, she purposely left home by 10:00 a.m. to run errands in Butte Creek and eat lunch at the small cafe near the bank. On the theory that the isolation of the ranch and her need to hear another human voice had driven her to seek out Zach the day before, she determinedly struck up conversations with the owner of the cafe and the librarian at the small, well-stocked city library. It was nearly three o'clock before she returned home to find Zach's pickup absent from its customary parking place in front of the shop.

"Good," she murmured with satisfaction. "It's just as well." She went up the porch steps, opened the front door and went inside.

The house seemed empty and too quiet. CeCe paused to switch on the stereo system, and the low growl of a saxophone filled the air. Angus woke from his nap on the sofa, yawned, stretched and padded after her into the kitchen.

"It's not that I'm afraid to spend time with him," she assured the tomcat as she emptied a grocery sack on the counter and opened the cupboard doors. "I think it's a good idea that we develop a nice, safe, friendly relationship for the baby's sake. I want the adults that are a part of her life to at least be polite to each other."

The problem was, she thought as she emptied a small bag of sugar into a glass canister, she really wasn't sure how safe any relationship with Zach would be for her. She was far too aware of him.

I'm an adult. I'll get over it, she told herself firmly. *I'm going to have to deal with him for the next twenty-plus years.* She smoothed a hand over her stomach. *I'm sure this wild attraction is caused by my hormones running amok because of you, Baby, and as soon as you're born, it will go away.*

Comforted, she turned back to the forgotten sugar sack and tossed it into the trash.

She spent an uneventful, quiet evening. When she heard the muted rumble of Zach's pickup the next morning, she walked to the window and waved hello.

He lifted a hand in brief salute and she moved away, returning to her loom.

Angus eyed her, his whiskers twitching.

"I'm being friendly, Angus," she told him, returning his unblinking stare. "Friendly but reserved. Nice, safe and friendly."

Angus blinked once, slowly, before he padded across the room and rubbed against her leg. CeCe stroked her hand the length of his back and closed her fingers around his tail, the thick fur brushing her palm as the tomcat pulled it slowly through her gently closed fist. He settled to the floor, propping his chin and front paws on her foot.

CeCe accepted the gesture of comfort and support and patted his head, scratching the wide space between his ears, before returning her attention to the loom. She quickly became absorbed in the pattern she wove and lost track of time. The hours flew by.

The swift rap of knuckles on the front door startled her and she jumped in surprise, Angus rumbling with annoyance when the reflex unceremoniously knocked him off her foot. She stood, pushing back her chair, and he stalked off in disgust to leap onto his favorite perch on the back of the sofa.

She twitched the curtain aside and looked out. Zach stood on the porch and she pulled open the door.

"Hi," she began, and sucked in a sharp breath, her eyes widening in dismay. "What have you done to yourself?"

"I cut my finger. Have you got a Band-Aid I can use?" He glanced down at his hand. Blood soaked the handkerchief wrapped around his palm and dropped in slow splats against the porch floor. He grimaced. "I'm getting blood on your porch—sorry."

"Oh, for Pete's sake." Impatient, CeCe caught his jacket sleeve and tugged him over the threshold into the warm entry hall. Still gripping his sleeve, she urged him down the hall to the kitchen and the sink.

She efficiently stripped him of his unbuttoned coat, tossed it across a chair and turned on the cold-water tap. Carefully, she unwrapped the handkerchief, wincing at the sight of the blood that oozed sluggishly from a nasty cut across his palm. "What happened?"

"I grabbed a piece of old pipe. It slipped out of my hand and the jagged side sliced my palm."

"Well, you need more than a Band-Aid, Zach." She cradled his hand in hers, turning it under the water while she carefully rinsed the blood from the cut and assessed the damage. "I think this needs stitches."

Zach bent forward, peering down at his palm. His chest touched her shoulder blades and he was abruptly aware of the slim body trapped between him and the counter. She moved slightly and the loose fall of her hair brushed against the underside of his chin, releasing a faint, perfumed scent that drifted upward. His nostrils flared, his body reacting with an all too familiar tightening, and he withdrew suddenly, easing back and away from her until their bodies touched only where her hand held his.

"No," he said gruffly. "It doesn't need stitches. I've had worse cuts—I'll just slap a Band-Aid on it and go back to work."

Frowning, CeCe half turned to look up at him and

for the first time realized how close he stood. She froze, her fingers tightening over his. For one long moment, her eyes were held captive by his, her senses filled with the faint scent of aftershave mixed with the sharp tang of machine oil and the unique, indefinable, subtle scent that she'd come to associate with Zach alone.

With an effort, she forced herself to ignore the impact he had on her. "I think you should see the doctor. I really think this needs to be closed with stitches."

"No." His jaw firmed stubbornly. "I haven't got time."

CeCe studied his set face and determined eyes for a moment before she sighed with exasperation and gave in. "All right," she conceded. "The Band-Aids are in the bathroom—I'll be right back." But first, she returned her attention to his hand. The tap water still trickled over his palm, but the flow of blood had slowed from the cold, and the water that dripped from his hand to swirl in the sink was pink instead of bright crimson. She released his hand and caught up a towel to dry her hands. "Keep it under the water," she directed.

"Yes, ma'am."

She shot him a swift, assessing glance, but his expression held no trace of the faint irony she'd heard in his voice. Without comment, she turned on her heel and left the kitchen. When she returned, she carried a bottle of hydrogen peroxide, a tube of antiseptic cream, a clean towel, a box of assorted bandages and a roll of white tape.

"All right," she said with businesslike efficiency as she set the items down on the counter next to the sink and unscrewed the cap from the peroxide. "Dry your hand." She held out a towel and watched him turn off the tap. Silently, he took the towel and blotted his hand dry before stretching out his forearm, palm up, over the sink. Just as silently, CeCe tipped the bottle, pouring the antiseptic over the wound. The clear liquid fizzed along the jagged line of the ugly gash and she glanced quickly at Zach. He didn't flinch or even draw a deep breath.

Carefully, she blotted the moisture from his palm before dabbing antiseptic cream over the cut and applying a gauze pad. Instead of Band-Aids, she used narrow white medical tape.

"There." She smoothed her thumb over the tape one last time and glanced up. "That's the best I can do, but I still think you should see a doctor and have it stitched."

"Nope. This is just fine." He curled his hand into a fist before flexing the fingers slowly. "Feels a lot better. Thanks."

"You're welcome." She turned back to the counter, busying herself with screwing the cap back on the peroxide bottle, closing the box of gauze and tucking the tape into its container.

Zach watched her, reluctant to leave. He glanced around the kitchen; feminine, homey touches had transformed the once-sterile room. Woven blue and cream cushions padded the wooden chairs pushed up to the table and small terra-cotta pots filled with herbs added living green color on the windowsill. Blue and cream curtains framed the window and matched the seat cushions.

A kettle steamed gently on the stove and his stomach whispered a low growl as he breathed in the tempting aroma of soup that had been teasing his senses ever since he'd entered the house.

"Something smells good," he commented.

CeCe looked up. He'd folded his arms across his chest, and he leaned casually against the countertop, booted feet crossed at the ankles. She ignored the alert signals her body instantly sent her and switched her gaze to the kettle on the stove.

"Chicken soup," she said, glancing at the clock above the refrigerator. "And it should be done—it's almost noon. Would you like some?" she asked politely, certain that he would refuse.

Zach considered saying no, but just as he opened his mouth to decline, his stomach growled again. Loudly. CeCe's gray eyes widened in surprise before amusement danced in their depths.

"I guess you'd know I'm lying if I said no," he said ruefully, rubbing his demanding midriff with one hand.

"I guess I would," she answered, a smile curving her mouth. She pointed at the table. "Sit down—I'll feed you."

Zach shot her a narrow-eyed glance, but she laughed and waggled her fingers in a shooing gesture. "Sorry, I couldn't resist. You have to admit, I owe you a few commands after all the ones you've given me."

Zach unfolded his arms and strolled to the table.

"All right," he conceded as he pulled out a chair and dropped into it. "But don't think you can get away with it again. I'm wounded at the moment."

CeCe rolled her eyes. "Yeah, right, wounded," she repeated. "Not to mention hungry."

"Well, that might have something to do with it," he drawled. She laughed, a low throaty chuckle that stroked lazy, enticing fingers up his spine, and turned her back on him.

Zach indulged his need to look at her while her back was to him. Faded jeans clung snugly to slim thighs and cupped the curve of her bottom while the white wool turtleneck sweater she wore was the perfect backdrop for the glossy fall of chestnut hair that swung against her shoulder blades. There was a smooth grace to her quick, efficient movements as she took bowls from the cupboard and removed the lid from the kettle, ladling out soup before she took spoons from a drawer. Bowl and spoon in hand, she turned away from the counter and Zach looked quickly away, switching his attention to the huge cat that chose that moment to stroll into the kitchen.

CeCe set a spoon, butter knife and the steaming bowl on the place mat in front of him and retrieved a loaf of French bread from the counter. She swiftly cut thick slices and set the bread and butter on the table.

"Don't wait for me," she told him, noticing that he had yet to taste the soup. He picked up his spoon. Satisfied, she returned to the ladle and her own bowl. He glanced up as she came back to the table, favoring her with one of his rare smiles. Her heart stuttered and her steps faltered momentarily before she slid into her chair.

"This tastes as good as it smells," he commented.

"Thank you," she said, smoothing her napkin over her lap and picking up her own spoon.

Silence reigned for several moments. Angus wound around CeCe's ankles and meowed demandingly. She glanced down and he halted immediately, sitting and eyeing her expectantly.

"You are such a beggar," she scolded him.

"He eats soup?" Zach asked.

"He eats *anything,*" CeCe said, eyeing the cat fondly. "But what he really wants is a bite of my bread—with lots of butter." She broke off a piece of soft bread and spread more butter on top. Angus meowed with throaty approval and CeCe lifted a paper napkin from the holder in the center of the table, spread it on the floor beside her chair and deposited the bite of bread.

Angus purred with rumbling appreciation, and with dainty precision demolished the bread.

"See?" CeCe glanced at Zach.

"Strange cat," Zach commented thoughtfully. "I don't think I've ever known a cat that eats bread and butter."

"I suspect he went hungry more than once when he lived in that Seattle alley," CeCe responded. "Which is probably why he eats just about anything I put in front of him. Although," she said, picking up her spoon, "he prefers fresh salmon from the Pike's Place Market."

"Mmm." Zach glanced at the cat's sleek coat and

well-padded frame. "Does he miss the comfort of the city?"

CeCe's gaze sharpened. "I don't think so—he's well fed." She paused. "I don't miss it, either."

"No?" Zach didn't betray his interest in her reply by so much as a lifted eyebrow.

"No," she said firmly. "I don't."

"You don't mind the snow?"

"No, I don't mind the snow. It's a nice change from the rain."

"And it doesn't bother you to live in the country instead of a town filled with people?" Zach had a hard time believing CeCe was adapting as well as she claimed.

"Ah, you've got me there." CeCe looked past him and out the kitchen window. "That's a mixed blessing. I love the quiet of the country. I definitely don't miss the sound of sirens that used to wake me in the middle of the night, nor do I regret that I no longer have to race through the pouring rain to catch the bus for work in the morning. But I have to confess that I miss having people to talk to. It's not as if I had dozens of close friends in the city, but everyday life there brought me into constant contact with people." Her gaze moved back to Zach and she smiled wryly. "Like most things in life, this is a good news–bad news situation. The good news is that here I have all the time and solitude I've wished for to work on my designs and the loom. The bad news is, I'm not used to having all this time to myself—with only myself and Angus for company."

"So you miss the bright lights?"

"No." she shook her head. "I don't miss the bright lights. I just get lonely for the sound of another human's voice. But if I ever do miss the city whirl," she added, "I'll go visit Dad and Mom for a week or two and indulge myself."

"Your folks live in Seattle?"

"Actually, they live in Bellevue," she clarified. "But it's only a short drive from the city across the floating bridge over Lake Washington."

"Oh." Zach was silent for a moment. "Your folks didn't mind that you moved so far away?"

"Goodness, no." CeCe looked at him in surprise. "I'm old enough to make my own decisions and live where I want."

Zach slowly scanned her features. Her fair, faintly tanned skin was creamy smooth and unlined, her soft mouth bare of lipstick, and he scowled. "You don't look old enough to be living in your own apartment, let alone hundreds of miles away from your parents."

CeCe gaped at him in astonishment before she burst out laughing. "I think I'll choose to take that as a compliment."

Zach's face heated, flushing faintly red across the high arch of his cheekbones. "I didn't mean it as an insult," he said uncomfortably.

"Good." Her eyes danced with amusement. "Because some men equate youth with stupidity when it comes to women."

Zach held up his hands, palms outward, and shook his head. "Not me," he vowed.

CeCe stared at him for a long moment. "If that's

true," she said, "why are you constantly telling me what I should and should not do?"

"I don't—" He began to speak, but halted when she arched one delicate, dark eyebrow in patent disbelief. "Well, maybe I do—sometimes," he conceded, ignoring her sniff of disagreement when he added the last word. "But it's not as if I normally tell the women I know what to do. I only do it with you because you're new to Montana, not to mention new to living in the country—which is a lot different than living in a big city like Seattle. Furthermore," he went on, "you're the only woman carrying a baby that I'm responsible for. If it weren't for that baby, I'd leave you alone to make your own mistakes."

"I don't believe you." She pointed her spoon at him. "I think you're one of those men who automatically takes over and tells the little woman—*any* woman—how to live her life, solely because you're bigger and stronger."

"That's ridiculous." Zach snorted in disgust. "Ask Jennifer or Sarah. I *never* get involved with women. I'm too busy."

Shocked, CeCe propped her chin on her fist and eyed him with interest. "You *never* get involved with women?"

"Hell, no," he said tightly. "Except for Jennifer and Sarah, most of you are more trouble than you're worth."

Her eyes danced with amusement. "No kidding? Why is that?"

"Because you're..." Zach halted in midsentence and glared at her, shaking his head. "Because you're sneaky, that's why. And stop changing the subject. I plan to continue watching you until you have this kid, and after that, till the kid's grown, if I have to. So you might as well get used to it.''

CeCe rolled her eyes. "Men," she said, sighing theatrically. "You can be such a pain."

"Yeah, well, so can you women," Zach retorted.

"Do you suppose we'll argue this much until Baby turns twenty-five?" she asked.

Her voice was almost wistful. Zach searched her face for clues to what she was feeling, but all he could read on her features was curiosity. "Probably," he answered bluntly.

She heaved a heavy sigh and picked up her spoon. "Well," she said with philosophical practicality, "then I guess I'd better get used to it." She glanced up just in time to see satisfaction flash across his face. "And you should get used to me ignoring you and doing as I choose."

He frowned, but before he could comment, she swallowed the last spoonful of her soup and pushed back her chair, glancing up at the clock as she folded her napkin and returned it to the blue and cream place mat.

"Time for me to get back to work," she said brightly, pointedly looking at his empty bowl before gathering up her silverware, soup bowl and bread plate, then crossing to the counter.

She set her handful of dirty dishes in the sink, squirted liquid detergent atop them and turned on the tap. Behind her, she heard his chair scrape back and the clatter of crockery, followed by the tread of boots against linoleum. She knew he stood behind her just before one brawny arm reached around her to slip bowl, plate, spoon and knife into the hot, soapy water.

"Thanks for lunch."

"You're welcome." She didn't turn, but he didn't move away. Every nerve ending in her body leaped, vibrating with awareness. With a start, she realized the hot water was about to overflow and she hastily turned off the tap.

Silence filled the kitchen. Still, he didn't move. Unable to endure the suspense, CeCe turned, pressing back against the counter as Zach leaned forward and rested his hands on the counter edge on either side of her, boxing her in.

"Just for the record," he said softly, "I don't take well to being ignored."

CeCe's eyes widened. "Are you threatening me?" she demanded.

"Nope," he said, his voice husky, deeper. "I never threaten."

His lashes lowered as his gaze left hers and moved slowly downward to fasten on her mouth. When the thick tawny brush of lashes lifted, his eyes held a sizzling heat that took her breath. For one heart-stopping moment, she was sure he was going to lower his head the few inches that separated them and cover her mouth with his. Her heart shuddered and she wanted the pressure of his lips against hers with a fierceness that shocked her.

His hands closed into fists where they rested on the countertop and he shoved away from her. He strode to the table and caught up his coat from the chair back where CeCe had tossed it. Heading for the door to the hall, he paused on the threshold and looked back at her.

"Thanks again for lunch."

His voice was still deeper, huskier, than normal, but his eyes had regained their cool reserve. CeCe nodded and he disappeared. She heard his footsteps down the hall, then the front door as it quietly opened and closed.

"Friendly," she muttered to herself as she turned back to the sink and began to scrub the dishes with uncharacteristic force. "Remember to keep this nice, friendly and safe."

It was three days later before the quiet house drove her back to the machine shop with a coffee cup in each hand. Fortunately, Zach didn't comment. Instead, he stopped working, sipped his coffee and responded when she asked him about the weather, the machinery he worked on and why Jennifer and Sarah didn't answer their phones. When she learned they'd gone to Billings for the week to visit friends, she sighed and made up her mind to visit Butte Creek and the library the next day.

The days moved slowly by. CeCe settled into a routine, working on her loom by day, knitting baby things at night. She became a regular visitor to the library, chatting with the librarian and checking out books to fill the long evening hours with reading.

Her midmorning coffee breaks with Zach became daily occurrences, as did shared lunches in her warm kitchen. An unspoken agreement kept their conversations on safe, noncontroversial ground, and CeCe grew to count on their daily conversations to lessen the isolation of the ranch.

Before she knew it, Thanksgiving arrived. She baked pumpkin pies, bundled herself into winter gear and drove to Jennifer and Lucas Hightower's ranch for the day.

Sarah Hightower answered CeCe's knock at the door.

"Hi." She smiled and held the door wide, shivering as the frosty air reached her. "Come in, come in. It's too cold to stand out there."

"You're right." CeCe stepped into the warm entryway and let Sarah take the pie carrier from her before she tugged her knit cap from her head and shrugged out of her coat and muffler, tucking her gloves into her coat pocket. "It's freezing."

Sarah reached for the coat, but CeCe shook her head. "Oh no you don't. Just tell me where to put it and I'll take it. I'm sure you shouldn't be lifting anything heavier than—what did Zach say? Oh, yes, a coffee cup."

Sarah groaned. "Zach spends too much time around my husband. I swear, by the time I have this baby, Josh will be refusing to let me lift even a cup."

"Well, maybe a half-full coffee cup," CeCe said teasingly.

"Just wait," Sarah said threateningly. "Zach is showing all the signs of being as impossible as Josh. And you aren't even waddling yet."

"True." CeCe glanced down at the blue wool that smoothed across her still nearly flat tummy. "No one would even know I was pregnant if I didn't tell them. Shouldn't I be showing, at least a little?''

"When did you conceive?" Sarah asked.

"Around July twentieth—which makes me four months," CeCe replied.

"Then it's not at all strange that you're not showing," Sarah reassured her. "Besides, isn't this your first pregnancy?"

"Yes."

"Well then, that explains it. Your stomach muscles are tight. I hardly showed at all with J.J. until I was nearly five months along." She stroked her palm caressingly over the mound of her belly. "But with this little one, I started wearing maternity clothes before I was three months pregnant."

"Really?" CeCe smiled with relief when Sarah nodded.

"Really." Sarah patted her shoulder. "Believe me, you should enjoy wearing your normal-size clothes as long as you can. You're going to get *so* tired of being three or four sizes larger than you are now."

"Three or four sizes? All over? I refuse to gain that much weight!"

"Don't worry, you won't—not as long as you continue watching your diet." Sarah waved CeCe ahead of her toward the kitchen.

They passed a wide archway and CeCe caught a quick glimpse of the living room. Zach stood on the far side of the room with a group of men listening to Josh Hightower. He glanced up, his gaze finding hers with unerring accuracy; emotion blazed swiftly in his eyes and was just as swiftly extinguished. He nodded in greeting before his attention returned to Josh.

The brief encounter lasted only seconds, but CeCe's heart thundered in her ears, and she realized that Sarah had asked something and was waiting for a reply.

"I'm sorry, Sarah," she apologized. "I'm afraid I didn't hear the question."

Sarah pushed open the swinging door to the kitchen and the mouthwatering aroma of baking turkey floated down the hallway. "I asked if your parents were disappointed that you couldn't make it home for the holiday?"

"No, they know I don't plan to visit them in Seattle until after the baby is born." She smiled affectionately. "They had mixed feelings about my marriage, but there's no question about how much they're looking forward to having a grandchild. I'm sure they'll be on the first plane leaving Seattle for Montana the moment they hear the baby is born."

Jennifer glanced over her shoulder as they stepped into the kitchen. "Hello, CeCe. You made it." She caught up a terry towel and dried her hands. "I want you to meet Annabel Fitch, our neighbor." A white-haired woman with keen eyes, her spare frame enveloped in a huge apron, waved a half-peeled carrot and smiled in greeting. "And this is my niece, Caitlin." Jennifer draped an arm over a teenage girl's shoulder and gave her a quick hug. The girl's green eyes lit with affection and she grinned at her aunt before nodding at CeCe.

"Hi." CeCe returned their friendly greetings. She

glanced at the bag of potatoes on the counter next to Caitlin. "Can I help with something? Peeling potatoes, maybe?"

"Absolutely," Caitlin said swiftly. "I *hate* peeling potatoes."

"But you love mashed potatoes, so remember when you're eating them that if the cook didn't peel them first, they'd never make it to your plate." Jennifer chuckled at Caitlin's grimace and handed an apron to CeCe. "Thanks, CeCe, I appreciate another pair of hands. As usual, the men are talking in the living room while the women are at work in the kitchen."

"Josh would help if you asked him," Caitlin said, clearly jumping to her uncle's defense.

"I know," Jennifer agreed, shooting her niece a fond look.

By the time dinner was on the table, CeCe felt as if she'd known Annabel and Caitlin for years rather than hours. Caitlin told CeCe that she had lived with Sarah and Josh since she was twelve years old and ran away from her mother's home in Los Angeles. CeCe found it difficult to reconcile the confident, mature teenager with the troubled child Caitlin painted.

Annabel Fitch was a delight. CeCe had no idea how old she was, but her dry wit and the twinkle in her eyes endeared her.

The long oak table was laden with food, and CeCe sat between Annabel and J.J., and directly across from Zach. Even separated by the width of the table, he exerted a pull on her senses that made the inevitable eye contact joltingly electric. Beside her, J.J. wiggled

impatiently while his uncle Lucas said grace and
CeCe welcomed the diversion offered by the active
little boy. The moment Lucas's "amen" was echoed
around the table, J.J. heaved a sigh of relief and
reached for a bowl of candied yams. CeCe offered
her own silent prayer of thanks and busied herself
with J.J.'s chattering, avoiding any casual glances
across the table at Zach.

It wasn't until dinner was over and the group of
family and friends had retreated to the living room
for coffee and dessert, that Sarah told CeCe about a
local rancher who raised sheep.

"Last year Duncan Burke bought six ewes and a
ram from a breeder. The wool is wonderful, CeCe.
You should talk to him about buying some for your
weaving."

CeCe's eyes lit with interest. "I'd love to. Do you
think you could introduce me? Would you have time
next week to take me to meet him?"

"I'd be glad to," Sarah responded. "But Duncan
is practically a recluse. I'm not sure I'm the best person to take you out there."

Disappointed, CeCe's face fell.

"But Zach knows him very well. In fact, he's probably one of the few friends Duncan has."

CeCe glanced across the room where Zach sat in
an upholstered chair with Stevie perched on his knee.
He smiled at the little boy, and CeCe's heart melted.

She wasn't at all sure that she should spend extra
time alone with him, but the lure of finding unique
wool was strong.

"Zach." Sarah's voice carried clearly across the

room. The rancher looked up, settling the restive Stevie more securely on his knee. "CeCe wants to meet Duncan Burke and see his sheep—the new ones he's experimenting with. Do you have time next week to run her out to his place?"

"Maybe." Zach's reply was purposely noncommittal. He glanced at CeCe, seated next to Sarah on the sofa, and frowned at the interest he read on her face. "You're *not* buying any of his sheep," he said bluntly.

CeCe bristled, stiffening. "I don't believe Sarah said I wanted to buy them," she said with emphasis. "Only that I wanted to look at them."

"I don't care if you look, just don't buy."

Heat bloomed in her cheeks. She bit back the sharp reply that trembled on her tongue and instead smiled sweetly. "I'll certainly take your advice under consideration, Mr. Colby, if I decide to purchase sheep in the future."

The smile that curved her lush mouth didn't reach her eyes. Instead, the irritation in her darkened gray eyes threatened him with retribution.

Chapter Six

Stevie wriggled to get down. Distracted, Zach steadied him while the boy slipped to the floor. Jennifer called her son and Zach glanced at her as Stevie raced across the room to wrap his arms around her legs. Jennifer's eyes danced with knowing, teasing mischief and Zach swiftly scanned the rest of the too-quiet group. Everyone within hearing distance had stopped conversing and was listening with open curiosity, clearly waiting with interest for his reply to CeCe's last comment.

"I'll be happy to drive you out to Duncan's place next week," he said tersely.

"Thank you." Her reply was carefully polite.

Zach knew that she would have liked to have thrown his offer to introduce her to Duncan back in his face. Only the presence of the interested listeners surrounding them prevented her from doing just that.

Beside her, Sarah touched CeCe's arm to claim her attention and she turned away from him to focus on Sarah.

"You know, Zach," Josh said quietly. "If I didn't know better, I'd swear there's something going on between you two."

Zach glanced sharply at Josh, but his friend returned his stare with a bland look that held only mild inquiry. "There's nothing between us but that damn will and her baby's inheritance," he muttered. "We can barely have a three-sentence conversation without arguing."

"Hmm." Josh nodded sagely. "I see."

"What does that mean?" Zach snapped, glaring at him.

"That means there's enough sparks flying between you and the pretty widow to start a brushfire."

"You're wrong," Zach denied brusquely. "And even if you weren't, she's Aaron's widow."

Josh sobered, the amusement disappearing from his eyes. "Yeah," he said. "That's not something you're likely to forget." Silence stretched for a long moment as both men watched the two women, Sarah's small-boned body ripe with pregnancy, CeCe's slenderness not yet revealing the child she bore.

"No," Zach said bleakly. "Not hardly."

He makes her laugh. Hands shoved in his jacket pockets, Zach listened to CeCe and Duncan Burke discuss the distinctive qualities of the wool from his six ewes. Duncan's normal reserve was absent, his craggy features softened with a rare smile, his dark eyes warm with approval as he watched CeCe praise and pet his favorite ewe. *And I haven't heard him talk this much in the ten years I've known him.* But then, he reflected, he himself had the same reaction to CeCe. There was something about her that made people open up.

CeCe laughed, her eyes bright with interest as Duncan described the antics of the mischievous, youngest ewe. As he talked, the ewe crowded closer to the tall rancher, butting her head against his jeans-clad knee in a bid for attention.

Duncan rubbed the sheep's ears with affection. "Feel her coat," he invited CeCe.

She buried her fingers in the thick wool.

"It seems very dense. My grandmother kept several sheep and I don't remember their coats feeling quite like this."

"I bought these sheep from Jay Asumendi—he's fifth-generation Basque, and for centuries his family has bred sheep specifically to produce high-quality wool."

"Basque?" CeCe asked with interest, looking more closely at the sheep. "Did you import Matilda from Europe?"

"No." Duncan shook his head. "Jay lives in Idaho, although the Asumendi family probably still has relatives in Spain or France."

"He certainly raises wonderful sheep," CeCe said wistfully, scratching the friendly pet ewe between the ears. "Zach…" She glanced up. "Couldn't we…"

"No."

She frowned at his brusque refusal and straightened, her fingers leaving the ewe's woolly head. "You haven't even heard what I'm going to ask," she protested.

"I know what you're going to say, and the answer is no," he said bluntly. "We're not raising sheep."

"I'm not suggesting we have a whole flock," she argued. "Just a few—maybe ten or twelve."

"No."

"Why are you so dead set against this?" she demanded, glaring at him. "What difference could a dozen or so sheep make on a ranch that has thousands of acres? You'll hardly know they're there."

"I'll know." Zach scowled back at her. "I told you before—I'm a cattle rancher. I do *not* raise sheep."

"You're prejudiced," she accused.

"Damn straight," he retorted.

CeCe threw up her hands in frustration. "You're impossible!"

Beside her, Duncan Burke chuckled.

Both CeCe and Zach turned to glare at him and he laughed outright, the rare smile lighting his taciturn, craggy features with amusement.

"Sorry," he said dryly.

"How can you be friends with someone as hardheaded and closed-minded as him?" CeCe demanded with irritation, gesturing at Zach.

"Well, shoot, ma'am," Duncan drawled, "I reckon he can't help it that he's too blind to recognize that sheep are far superior to cattle. I figure he was probably brainwashed by his granddad, who was a hard-headed cattleman.''

"Oh, for—'' Zach bit off a cussword and glared at his friend. "If you weren't so damned stubborn, you'd get rid of these mangy sheep and run cattle, like every other rancher in the county that has half a brain.''

"You cattlemen are all alike," Duncan replied. "Too used to wrangling mule-headed cattle to recognize the benefits of herding sheep.''

Zach's response to the argument that he'd had so often with Duncan was forestalled by the strident ring of the phone mounted on the shed wall near the outer door. Duncan walked past him and spoke briefly before silently holding the phone out toward him. Surprised, Zach strode across the shed and took the receiver.

"Hello."

Alarmed, CeCe saw Zach stiffen, his face reflecting shock, followed swiftly by a flash of fear, before all emotion was wiped from his features.

"I'm on my way," he said tersely. He replaced the phone with a quick snap and shoved one hand into his pocket, pulling out a ring of keys that included the ignition key to the truck.

"What's wrong?" CeCe asked.

"Sarah's gone into labor.''

"But she isn't due yet, is she?''

"Not for another few weeks," Zach answered grimly. His gaze met Duncan's. "We'll have to finish this argument some other time, Duncan. I'm going to the hospital.''

"No problem." Duncan strode ahead of them, shouldering open the heavy shed door. "Tell Josh I'm hoping for the best."

"I will." Zach nodded to Duncan and caught CeCe's arm in a firm grip, hustling her across the snowy ground to his pickup. He yanked open the door and didn't bother waiting for her to climb in. Instead, he grabbed her at the waist and lifted her onto the high seat. "Buckle up," he said, and slammed the door.

Zach didn't speak again until they reached the end of the long, snow-covered ranch road. He braked, the big truck easing to a stop at the edge of the wider county road, and looked at CeCe. To the left was the Hall ranch, to the right lay the shortest route to the hospital at Butte Creek.

"Do you mind going with me to the hospital?" he asked. "I'll take you home as soon as I talk to Josh and find out how Sarah and the baby are doing."

"I'd much rather go with you," she quickly assured him. "If you take me home, I'll just sit by the telephone and worry until I know that Sarah and the baby are safe and well."

Zach nodded and swung the pickup to the right, accelerating the moment the wheels caught traction on the gravel. CeCe's fingers gripped the armrest on the door and she uttered a silent prayer for safety as they sped toward Butte Creek. Beside her, Zach was silent also, concentrating on driving, and she cast a sideways glance at him. Beneath the brim of his black cowboy hat, his eyes were narrowed as he scanned the stretch of highway before them, his lips set in a grim line.

The weak afternoon sunlight was already failing as they walked swiftly through the doors of the hospital. The delivery rooms were on the second floor and Zach didn't bother waiting for the elevator. Instead, he caught CeCe's hand in his and drew her with him up the stairs. His long legs took the steps easily, but CeCe was out of breath when they reached the second floor. Jennifer and Lucas stood outside a waiting room halfway down the long hall and CeCe struggled to match Zach's long strides as he moved swiftly toward them.

"How is she?" Zach demanded, his voice pitched low in deference to the hospital's muted sounds.

"Fine," Lucas reassured him. "The doctor told Josh that although the baby's arriving a few weeks early, Sarah's labor is perfectly normal. He can't guarantee an easy delivery, but he doesn't foresee any problems at the moment."

Zach's iron grip on CeCe's fingers eased and he drew a deep breath, his forehead clearing. "Thank God," he said quietly.

CeCe sighed with relief, her fingers clinging unconsciously to the strength of his. Zach responded by squeezing her hand reassuringly.

"Where's Josh?" he asked, glancing down the empty hall beyond Lucas and Jennifer.

"He's in the labor room with Sarah," Jennifer said. "Murphy and Charlie are in the waiting room. Lucas and I just called home to check in with Caitlin and the boys.''

"There's a coffeepot with halfway decent coffee in there," Lucas offered.

"Good." A half grin lifted Zach's mouth. "I could use some. I don't know how you and Josh get through this," he added. "I'm only an honorary uncle and I'm worried."

"Tell me about it," Lucas said with a shake of his head. "It's bad enough when it's my sister-in-law. When Jennifer was in labor, I was a nervous wreck."

"Yes, but you survived." Jennifer slipped her hand through the crook of her husband's elbow and led him toward the waiting-room doorway. "And so did I. And so will Sarah," she added.

Zach looked down at CeCe. Her profile was to him as she watched Jennifer and Lucas walk away, the lines of her forehead, nose, lips and chin cameo perfect in the bright hospital lighting. The other couple disappeared through the doorway and she glanced up at him. Apprehension lurked in the darkened gray depths of her eyes.

"What's wrong?" he asked.

Her gaze left his to flicker down the hall and back again. "This is the first time I've been in an obstetrics ward since I've been pregnant. Oh, I've had friends who had babies, so it's not like I've *never* been in a hospital delivery wing before," she hastened to add. "But knowing that in a few months I'll be going through what Sarah is now—" She shrugged helplessly, unable to put into words precisely what she was feeling. "It's different somehow. Scary—but awesome."

Zach wanted to pull her close and shield her, reassure her that she'd be okay—that he'd keep her safe. He restrained the urge, just barely.

"Yeah," he said gruffly, trying to think of a way to reassure her without touching her. "Maybe it's a good thing that you can see Sarah go through this. Would you like to stay until the baby's born? I'll take you home now if you want, but you're welcome to wait with us and see the baby, maybe talk to Sarah afterward."

"I'd like that." She was relieved that he'd suggested it. There were times when her pregnancy made her emotions seesaw, and to her chagrin this was one of those times. Because she craved the security of the callused warmth of his hand closed around hers and wanted badly to cling to him, she purposely forced her fingers to loosen. She tugged gently, but he didn't release her. She glanced down at their linked hands, and tried to ignore the wave of emotion that swept her as she stared at his much larger hand holding hers.

Zach's gaze followed hers and he realized that he held her hand wrapped in his. The contact point of softness and warmth sent a jolt of reaction through him. He released her fingers with sudden swiftness. Her gaze flew up to meet his and he steeled himself against the inquiry he read there.

"I need a cup of coffee," he said abruptly.

CeCe stared at him for a moment before she smiled wryly. "I hope the hospital has herbal tea," she commented, turning toward the waiting room.

"If there isn't any on this floor, I'll go down to the cafeteria and find you a cup," Zach promised, following her.

The afternoon wore slowly on for the six people in the waiting room. They took turns flipping the channels on the television set, refilling the coffeemaker, rereading the dog-eared magazines, playing gin rummy, pacing the hall and checking at the nurses' station for status reports. At seven o'clock in the evening, Jennifer returned from a trip to the station with the welcome news that Sarah had been taken to the delivery room.

A sigh of collective relief filled the room.

"It's about time," Zach muttered.

CeCe glanced at him. He was slouched on the sofa, his long, blue-jean-clad legs stretched out in front of him, boots crossed at the ankle, head resting against the back of the low sofa. He'd been reading, and the magazine lay across the flat plane of his midriff, the bright cover a splash of color against the muted blue of his denim shirt.

Her body sent her an unmistakable surge of desire. *What lousy timing,* she lectured herself wryly. Determinedly, she turned her attention and her eyes back to the sitcom rerun on the television screen.

Another forty-five minutes ticked slowly past before Josh appeared in the doorway. Still wearing a green hospital gown over his shirt and jeans, his hair rumpled as though he'd plowed worried fingers through its thickness, he looked tired and immensely happy.

"Hey," he said, his broad grin widening as all five adults turned swiftly. "What are you doing in here? Why aren't you down the hall at the nursery window waiting to see the latest addition to the Hightower clan?"

"Josh!" Jennifer ran across the room and caught his arm. "Are they both all right? Is the baby a boy or a girl?"

"Yes, they're fine, just fine," Josh reassured her. "And it's a he—a little boy, seven pounds, three ounces, twenty-one inches long."

"Congratulations, Dad." Lucas engulfed his brother in a swift, hard hug.

"Where's my cigar?" Zach asked Josh, clapping him on the shoulder.

"I haven't bought cigars yet," Josh told him. "But I will."

"Good," Murphy drawled. "Make sure they're the thickest, smelliest ones you can find. It drives the women crazy, but they can't say much because cigars and births are a tradition."

Charlie laughed, his eyes twinkling with amusement.

"Men," Jennifer said with feigned disgust. She tugged on Josh's arm. "Let's go see this baby."

They trooped out of the room, CeCe and Zach bringing up the rear. The nurse obligingly wheeled the bassinet close to the window so the group gathered outside the nursery could say hello to little Justin Hightower.

"His hair is black, Josh," Jennifer said softly. "Just like his daddy's."

"I wonder if he has his daddy's eyes?" Murphy commented, peering closely through the glass.

"I can't tell," Josh answered. "I know they're dark blue, but I'm not sure about the shape. Ask Sarah, maybe she knows."

"What room is she in?" Jennifer asked.

"Two-twenty, right down the hall."

"Can she have visitors yet?"

"Sure," Josh replied. "I promised her that we'd be in to see her after you had a chance to say hello to Justin."

"Good." Jennifer tugged Lucas away from the window. "Let's go tell her what a beautiful baby she has."

Murphy, Charlie and Josh followed Jennifer and Lucas down the hall. CeCe remained at the nursery window, Zach at her elbow, smiling mistily through the glass at the newborn. The baby yawned, his little face scrunching up in a comical grimace, tiny fists flailing the air as he wriggled and stretched.

"Isn't he beautiful?" CeCe's voice was hushed, bemused as the baby settled, his lashes lifting slowly to reveal navy blue eyes.

"Beautiful?" Dubious, Zach eyed the tiny scrap of humanity. "He's kind of wrinkled, don't you think?"

"Only a little."

"He's got a lot more hair than Lucas and Jennifer's boys did," Zach commented, smiling gently as Justin brought his knees to his chest before stretching out his legs in a convulsive, kicking movement.

"Really?" CeCe touched her fingertips and palm against the glass, wishing she could hold the baby.

Justin's thick hair lay in a black cap against his small skull, curving behind his ears. "He has perfect little ears, doesn't he?" she whispered.

"And fingers," Zach agreed. Justin yawned again and batted at the air with one little fist. "Look how tiny his hand is—and his arm."

CeCe nodded. "He's amazing, isn't he?"

"He's a miracle," Zach agreed soberly. "Josh was afraid he might not get here at all. Sarah was hospitalized twice while she was pregnant."

Startled, CeCe glanced swiftly at Zach. He was staring solemnly at Justin's tiny, blanket-covered shape. "I didn't know—what happened?"

"I'm not sure. Josh told me that she had a problem with high blood pressure. The doctor was worried about both her and the baby."

CeCe's gaze searched his. Gone was the cool, distant expression that habitually dwelt in his eyes. Now the silvery blue had darkened to slate, the memory of Sarah's danger chasing the remoteness from his features.

"But they're both all right now, aren't they?" she murmured. She held her breath, waiting for his answer.

"Josh said the doc gave them both a clean bill of health." His gaze flicked to the tiny figure in the bassinet beyond the glass before returning to hers. "But given her history—I was worried when Murphy called to tell me that she'd gone into labor early."

"Oh." CeCe nodded. For a man who claimed that women were more trouble than they were worth, Zach Colby obviously cared deeply for Sarah. A swift stab of regret that his concern didn't extend to her pierced her. She turned back to Justin and was swiftly distracted. "Then he truly is a miracle," she said softly.

"I suppose most babies are," Zach said thoughtfully, almost to himself.

She glanced up and his gaze dropped to meet hers. A gentle smile curved her mouth, her hand lifting to rest unconsciously, protectively, against her midriff. Her gray eyes were misty with awed emotion, and for once Zach ignored the warning bells that demanded he pull back. The sense that they were the only two people on earth who felt the enormity and wonder of this moment reached him on some deeply profound level.

What was it about this woman, he wondered, *that made him acknowledge feelings he'd never spoken aloud to another soul?*

The First Lutheran Church in Butte Creek was decorated for Christmas. Seated in the third pew from the front, between Annabel Fitch and Charlie, CeCe joined the congregation as they lifted their voices in the last verse of "Adeste Fidelis." In the far right corner at the front of the church, a tall evergreen glowed with colored lights, its broad branches festooned with garlands, tinsel and brilliant-colored glass balls that reflected the light. Potted poinsettias banked the altar railing, their velvety red and green leaves a colorful counterpoint to the white-and-gold altar cloth.

In the pew in front of CeCe, Justin stirred in his mother's arms, fussing with little squirms and muted grumblings. Sarah cuddled him closer, murmuring softly, and he quieted. CeCe smoothed her palm over the outward swell of her tummy beneath her red wool dress. Only a little more than four months to wait and she would have a tiny bundle of her own to cuddle and soothe, she thought with dreamy anticipation.

Her gaze moved over Josh, seated next to Sarah, and beyond him to Zach. The conventional black western suit he wore with a white shirt fit smoothly across the breadth of his shoulders. He hadn't worn his black Stetson into the church, and his tawny hair gleamed a dull gold. He tilted his head to the right to hear a whispered comment from Murphy, and for an all too brief moment she saw his sculpted profile against the dark green of the Christmas tree.

Annabel nudged her discreetly and CeCe hastily rose with the congregation to receive the end-of-service blessing. The minister finished, smiled benignly and asked them to be seated, inviting the congregation to share in the christening of little Justin Hightower.

"Will the parents and godparents bring Justin to the altar?"

Sarah and Josh rose, Jennifer and Zach following them as they left the pew and made their way down the aisle to the front of the church.

The service that followed was solemn, broken only by Justin's happy gurgles as Sarah transferred him to Jennifer's arms. Unafraid, the baby stared up at the minister with wide eyes, babbling nonsensically as the adults voiced their parts in the proceedings. In fact, Justin's little face didn't crinkle into a frown until everyone gathered in the church's basement social room for coffee and cake to celebrate the occasion.

"What's wrong, sweetheart?" Sarah cooed soothingly, taking the baby from Josh's arms. The long, white christening gown hung far past his booties, trailing over her arm as she cradled him close.

"I think he's tired," Caitlin offered, touching a fingertip to the baby's petal-soft cheek.

"He was an angel all during the christening," Annabel commented. "And he was so cute when he grabbed the minister's finger."

"He was trying to chew on it," Josh said dryly. "I think he's hungry."

"He can have my cake, Daddy," J.J. offered, standing on tiptoe to peer at his new little brother's face.

"Thanks, slugger." Josh affectionately tousled J.J.'s silvery mop of hair. "But Justin is a little young for cake."

"I'll find someplace a bit more private," Sarah commented, glancing around the crowded room.

CeCe sipped her punch, only half listening to Annabel relate a story to Lucas and Josh. Zach stood on the far side of the room, one hand tucked in the pocket of his slacks, the other hand holding a glass of fruit punch, while he listened gravely to the minister chat.

In the weeks that she'd lived in Butte Creek, she'd heard more than one tale that involved the escapades of Zach Colby and the Hightower brothers when the three had been younger—and much wilder. Jennifer had confided in CeCe that she suspected Zach considered himself a social outcast because of the circumstances of his birth. It was clear to CeCe, however, after watching the warmth with which the congregation members greeted him and the respect with which they listened when he spoke, that the community felt a great deal of respect, admiration and affection for the big rancher.

"...aren't you, CeCe?"

Annabel's query caught CeCe's attention and she swiftly returned her regard to the group she stood with.

"I'm sorry...I'm afraid I didn't catch the question."

The wry, knowing look Annabel gave her brought a swift tide of color to CeCe's cheeks.

"I was telling Lucas how much I enjoyed Thanksgiving—and how much I'm looking forward to celebrating Christmas Eve at the Hightowers', especially now that there's a new baby. Don't you agree?"

"Yes," CeCe said with conviction, now that she knew what the question was. "I wouldn't miss it for the world. I love Christmas, and I'm already starting to feel blue that I'll be so far away from my parents and sister over the holidays."

"You're a close family?" Annabel asked.

"Very." CeCe nodded emphatically. "I'm sure my parents wish I hadn't decided to move to another state, but they want me to be happy and they're determined to make the best of it. Mom told Dad to look on the bright side—they'll have a new place to vacation and he'll have different fishing spots to test his skills. Still," she said wistfully, "I'm very glad

I've made such good friends in Butte Creek. This will be the first time I haven't been home for Christmas."

Annabel patted her arm consolingly. "We'll just have to make sure you're too busy to be lonely."

CeCe smiled and glanced past her. Her gaze collided with Zach's and a jolt of pure adrenaline raced through her veins.

If I were home in Washington for Christmas, I wouldn't spend Christmas Eve at the Hightowers' with Zach. Dismayed, she realized that she would miss Zach if she left Montana for the holidays just as much as she would miss her family by staying in Butte Creek.

She swallowed a groan and forced her gaze away from Zach's.

The ten days between Justin's christening and Christmas Eve flew by. CeCe had had little time to feel homesick for her parents and friends in Washington; she was kept busy finishing a special Christmas order from the exclusive women's shop in Seattle that marketed her weaving. She was looking forward to Christmas Eve at the Hightowers'.

Jennifer and Lucas's home smelled like Christmas. CeCe slipped through the throng of laughing party guests to reach the decorated fir tree at the far end of the long room. The pungent smell of evergreen mingled with the scent of bayberry candles, the muted glow of colored lights that draped the tree echoed by the candlelight's gleam. Atop an antique oak credenza, fat red and white candles were surrounded by evergreen boughs, colored glass Christmas balls tucked among the greenery reflecting the candle glow. The huge oak-framed mirror hanging above the credenza reflected the crowded room. The party-goers were all ages and sizes, dressed in Christmas finery.

"Lovely tree, isn't it?"

CeCe turned and found a petite, older woman behind her. Beautifully dressed in a conservative red suit with pearls, the woman's resemblance to Sarah Hightower was striking.

"Yes, it is." CeCe smiled and held out her hand. "I don't believe we've met. I'm Cecelia Hawkins."

"I'm Patricia Drummond," the older woman replied, taking CeCe's hand. "And although we haven't been formally introduced, I've heard a great deal about you. I'm Sarah's mother."

"Of course. I saw you at the christening but didn't get a chance to say hello. Sarah said you had to leave early to take several ladies home," CeCe said warmly. "And I understand that I just missed meeting you at the hospital when Justin was born."

"Yes. I was out of town and rushed back when Sarah went into labor. Unfortunately, I arrived at the hospital after all the excitement was over and Justin and Sarah were sleeping peacefully."

"Well, you have a beautiful new grandson," CeCe said warmly.

"Thank you. I think so too. I understand you're expecting a child of your own within a few months," Sarah's mother commented.

"Yes," CeCe confirmed. She wondered briefly if Mrs. Drummond knew the circumstances of the elder Mr. Hall's will. *Probably not*, she decided. The older woman's expression held no censure, only friendly interest. "Holding Justin makes me more impatient than ever for my baby to get here. I can't wait." She glanced down and smoothed a hand over the small, outward curve of her tummy.

Mrs. Drummond's gaze followed hers and she smiled understandingly. "I know what you mean, but have patience. By the time nine months passed, I felt as if I'd been pregnant forever, but it was all worth it when I held my girls."

"Hello!"

Caitlin Drummond, her black hair and green eyes set off by an emerald wool dress, slipped a hand through the crook of her grandmother's arm and smiled sunnily at the two women.

"Hello, Caitlin." Patricia lifted a slender hand and brushed her granddaughter's long hair back over one shoulder, narrowing her gaze over Caitlin's dainty ear where an intricately carved silver hoop dangled.

"I'm only wearing one pair of earrings, Grandmother." Caitlin's eyes danced with amusement. "But only because it's Christmas and I wanted to thank you for giving me this dress—which I love— as an early present."

Mollified, Patricia nodded abruptly. "I'm glad you like it, and green is an excellent color for you, child."

"Thank you, Grandmother." Caitlin glanced at CeCe. "I need to steal CeCe away from you. There's something I want her to see."

"Really? What?" CeCe asked.

"It's a secret," Caitlin responded. She released her

grandmother and caught CeCe's bare forearm, tugging gently. "Come with me."

CeCe shrugged and smiled at Patricia, letting the teenager draw her across the room to the doorway.

"Stand right here and don't move," Caitlin cautioned her.

"Aren't you going to tell me what this is all about?" CeCe asked, laughing at the suppressed excitement on Caitlin's vivid face.

"No, it's a surprise."

"Do I have to close my eyes?" CeCe asked.

"No, just stand there." Caitlin hurried through the doorway. "Don't turn around!" she said swiftly as CeCe half turned to watch her.

"How long do I have to stand here?" CeCe called over her shoulder.

"You can turn around now."

Laughing, CeCe turned. Caitlin stood directly behind her with both hands grasping Zach's arm. He wore dark dress slacks and a cream pullover sweater over a white shirt. CeCe had seen him earlier and said a brief hello, but the holidays had made her emotions even more erratic, so she'd avoided him after that first greeting. Now he eyed her with confusion, his expression mirroring her own puzzlement.

"Is this the surprise?" she asked Caitlin.

"Yes." Caitlin lifted one hand to point at the door frame above CeCe's head. "You're standing under the mistletoe."

CeCe glanced upward and, sure enough, a ball of greenery hung suspended from a glittery gold ribbon.

She looked back at Caitlin and Zach just in time to see comprehension flash in his blue eyes.

"Caitlin…" she began in protest.

"No excuses," the teenager said firmly, shaking her head and laughing. "Come on, Zach, you have to kiss her and wish her Merry Christmas."

Zach didn't want to touch her. He had the uneasy feeling that if he did, he wouldn't be able to let her go.

Behind him, Murphy's gravelly voice joined Caitlin's. "Caitlin's right. You have to kiss her. Come on, boy."

"Hurry up, Zach," Charlie said, joining Murphy's teasing.

CeCe couldn't read Zach's intention. The enigmatic shield that he wore so effortlessly had dropped over his face and even his eyes held no flicker of emotion. Several seconds ticked by. A flush of heat moved up her throat to stain her cheeks as she realized with dismay that he was going to refuse.

Zach gazed at CeCe. The swift color that flooded her cheeks was accompanied by a flash of hurt in the darkened gray depths of her eyes. He hadn't meant to hurt or embarrass her and, clearly, his hesitation had done both. Zach slipped his arm from Caitlin's loose hold and he took the one short step that brought him close to CeCe, close enough to brush against the white wool of her skirt. He slipped an arm around the curve of her waist.

"I never pass up an opportunity to kiss a beautiful woman," he said loud enough for his audience to hear. Then he bent his head and brushed her mouth with his.

CeCe's senses were on overload from the sudden, firm possessiveness of his arm around her waist. She didn't have time to prepare herself for the reality of his mouth against hers. The contact was brief, but the warm caress of his lips against hers sent her heart shuddering, and her head reeled dizzily when he released her.

Zach kept his eyes open, so he knew that CeCe's lashes had drifted shut for the brief seconds that their lips touched. Her lips were soft and lush, and he badly wanted to prolong the contact, but he forced himself to release her. When he did, her lips clung, her lashes lifting slowly to reveal dazed gray eyes.

Hell, he thought savagely, *why did this have to happen with half a dozen people looking on. I want her alone someplace. Anyplace.*

He forced his fingers to free her and he slid his arm from around her waist, lingering for a heartbeat to steady her when he felt the faint shudder that rippled through her slim body. For one long moment, his gaze met hers and then he stepped away from her, glancing at Caitlin with a forced half grin.

"I think you're next, Caitlin. Where's Trey?"

"No!" the teenager shrieked, held up her hands to ward him off and turned to flee.

"Oh no you don't!" Zach caught her around the waist and held her captive easily while Murphy scanned the room for the young man.

Grateful that Zach had diverted the laughing

crowd's attention away from her, CeCe took the opportunity to slip away into the kitchen.

"Hi, come join us." Jennifer gestured CeCe forward. She was seated at the table, munching on an iced sugar cookie, while across from her, Sarah fed Justin.

This room was quieter, the murmur of voices and Christmas carols from the living room interrupted by occasional bursts of laughter.

"Thanks." CeCe dropped into a chair and propped her elbows on the tabletop, gazing with fascination at the top of Justin's tiny head. "I think there's another Hightower with a hollow leg," she commented, watching the baby's cheeks move in and out as he sucked rhythmically.

"I think you're right," Sarah answered fondly, brushing a fingertip over the petal softness of the baby's cheek. "But I don't mind. I'm just glad he's here, safe and sound."

"I can't wait until I can say the same," CeCe said. "Unfortunately, I have three months, twenty-five days and twelve hours to go before I'm sure that Baby is healthy and well."

Jennifer paused with her cookie halfway to her open mouth and stared at CeCe in surprise. "My goodness, I always counted months, and sometimes days, but you have this down to hours? How can you be so sure?"

CeCe shrugged. "Because I know exactly what month, day and time I went to the clinic. So, of course, when the doctor told me the procedure was a success and that a normal gestation period lasts a certain number of days, it was only a matter of doing the math to calculate the birth date."

Sarah frowned in confusion. "But how did the doctor know exactly what day, time and hour you conceived? You must have kept exceptionally good records."

"Not me—the clinic," CeCe explained. Still Sarah and Jennifer looked at her without comprehension and she realized with a start that they couldn't possibly know she hadn't used traditional methods to become pregnant. "Oh, I'm sorry. I never told you, did I? I conceived at the clinic. Long before we married, Aaron became too ill to father a child normally. However, he wanted a child as desperately as I did and contributed sperm to a sperm bank. After we married, I became pregnant with the help of a wonderful doctor and his staff at a fertility clinic in Seattle."

Sarah and Jennifer's faces held a mix of surprise and amazement.

In the shadowed hall just outside the doorway, Zach Colby stood frozen, stunned by CeCe's calmly spoken words.

Chapter Seven

Aaron couldn't get her pregnant. Did he try? Exactly what kind of a marriage did they have?

Zach remembered all too well that his half brother had been more than willing to climb into bed with any available female in Butte Creek. He, himself, couldn't imagine being married to CeCe and not taking her to bed. But had Aaron?

It was nearly an hour before Zach finally followed CeCe into the kitchen and had her alone.

CeCe heard the door close behind her, glanced over her shoulder and stiffened with apprehension when she saw the look on his face. She turned slowly to face him. "Hello, Zach," she said warily.

He stalked across the kitchen floor toward her and she shifted closer to the counter at her back, glancing past him at the closed door, then back to search his set, determined expression. She wondered uneasily if he was angry with her for Caitlin's prank earlier. "Is something wrong?"

He kept walking until only inches separated their bodies and CeCe had to tilt her head back to maintain eye contact.

"Were you really married to Aaron?" he asked.

CeCe blinked in surprise. "Yes," she said. "Of course I was—why would you ask?"

"I overheard you tell Sarah and Jennifer that you got pregnant in a clinic," he said bluntly.

"Oh," CeCe narrowed her eyes at him. "You were eavesdropping."

"It wasn't planned. I was on my way to the kitchen to get a towel to mop up J.J.'s spilled eggnog and happened to be outside in the hall when you told Jennifer how you got pregnant."

"And leaped to the conclusion that I wasn't really married to Aaron?" Slowly rising temper that he doubted her honesty colored her words.

"No. If Aaron didn't get you pregnant, I can't help wondering what else Aaron did, or didn't, do with you."

"What do you mean by that?" she snapped, incredulous.

"What kind of a marriage did you have? People get married for lots of different reasons. Why did you marry him?"

Too taken aback by his blunt question to prevaricate, CeCe answered just as bluntly, "To have a child."

A flame leaped to life in his eyes. "Are you telling me you weren't in love with him?"

"We were friends," she said firmly. "He was very ill and..."

Zach caught her chin in his hand, cutting off her words. "Did you sleep with him?" he demanded fiercely, impatiently.

Too startled to be infuriated at his question, CeCe stared wide-eyed at the emotion that blazed from his eyes. "No. No, I didn't," she managed to get out, stumbling over the words. "He was too ill...he couldn't. And I wouldn't have wanted to, because we didn't have that kind of relationship. Why do—"

She didn't get to finish the sentence. Zach slid his arm around her waist and pulled her away from the counter, his mouth dropping to take hers with swift, fierce possession.

The kiss wasn't tentative, it wasn't sweet. It was hot, hungry and fueled by weeks of wanting and wondering and denying. Telling him to stop never occurred to CeCe. She'd dreamed about him for weeks and the reality was far better than her imagination. She slid her arms around his neck and pressed closer, the soft curves of her body fitting perfectly against the harder angles of his. Even the small, solid mound that was her tummy seemed shaped just to fit him.

He groaned, his arms tightening. His fingers fisted in her hair, the pressure of his mouth forcing her head back against his shoulder as the kiss turned hotter, feeding the hunger that grew the longer he held her.

CeCe forgot where she was, forgot everything beyond the frantic tide of heat and need that had her clinging to Zach, accepting and returning the hot pressure of his mouth with greedy delight. When he stiffened, his body going still before his mouth left hers, she murmured a protest, her lips clinging to his.

"Somebody's coming," he muttered, his voice gravelly with frustrated passion. CeCe stared up at him uncomprehendingly, her gray eyes smoky and heavy, her mouth faintly bruised-looking from the pressure of his. His fingers clenched over the curve of her shoulders and he battled the need to pull her close again. Reason won out and he set her away from him and left the room just as a group of merry guests pushed open the hall door.

CeCe spun to face the counter, staring blindly at the sink and the half-full tumbler of water for a full minute before remembering that the glass of water was the original reason she'd come to the kitchen. Hands trembling, she turned on the tap and held her fingers beneath the flow of water. Icy cold, the water helped to shock her and chase away the drugged state of her senses. She drew a deep, shaky breath, filled her glass and managed to make her way out of the room, unsure whether her vague smile and replies to the guest's comments made the slightest bit of sense. She collected her coat from the piled-high bed in Lucas and Jennifer's bedroom and drove home.

Angus greeted her return with appreciative, throaty purrs, winding around her ankles as she shed her coat and kicked off her shoes. She bent and picked him up, snuggling his furry head beneath her chin as she padded down the darkened hall to her bedroom. The lamp she'd left burning beside the bed lit the room with a warm, soft glow and she set Angus down atop the rose-colored comforter. He meowed companionably and curled up, watching her with unblinking gold eyes.

She undressed methodically, neatly hanging up her white wool dress before pulling a nightgown over her head. She paused in front of the mirror, turned sideways and smoothed the pink-rosebud-sprinkled white flannel over her midsection. The small curve of her belly brought a smile to her face and she patted it gently before turning away and climbing into bed.

Angus grumbled when the bed dipped under her weight and moved closer to curl against her legs. CeCe propped pillows behind her, picked up a new book on weaving from the nightstand and reached absently to smooth her palm over Angus's thick fur. "I wish all males were like you, Angus," she said, smiling as the tomcat stretched and purred beneath her stroking. "You're predictable and accommodating. As long as I feed you and keep you warm, you're perfectly happy. Human males, on the other hand, aren't anywhere near as simple to satisfy."

She wondered if Zach would ever be predictable or accommodating, or even remotely simple to satisfy. She doubted it. She already knew that he was autocratic, argumentative and not given to compromise. Since kissing him, she strongly suspected that any woman lucky enough to have him as a lover would find him intense, passionate and deeply satisfying. *Simple,* however, was not a word that she would ever consider applying to Zach Colby.

She refused to consider the possibility that the powerful force that drew her to him might be more than pregnancy-induced, rioting hormones. However, that refusal didn't keep her from dreaming in vivid Technicolor, reliving those all-too-brief moments in Jennifer Hightower's kitchen when his mouth had taught her things about kissing she'd never known before.

CeCe woke the next morning, feeling dissatisfied and frustrated, and when Zach knocked on the front door, she had mixed feelings about whether or not she should let him in.

"Oh, bother," she muttered. It was just a kiss. Why should she feel nervous about facing him?

She yanked open the door—and knew immediately why she was nervous. Seeing him had the same bone-melting effect as always, only now it was more intense.

"Good morning," she said.

"Morning." He eyed her silently for a moment. "Can I come in?"

"Oh. Certainly." She stepped back, and with two long strides Zach was past her and in the entryway. She closed the door and turned to face him. He'd pulled off his Stetson and was turning it, end over end, in his hands. If she didn't find it impossible to imagine, she'd think he was nervous.

"We need to talk," he said abruptly.

"All right," she said warily. "Do you want to come into the kitchen and sit down?"

Zach didn't want to go anywhere with her. He wanted to tell her the decision he'd reached after a long, nearly sleepless night, hear her agree and then get the hell out of her house and away from the temptation that was CeCe Hawkins. She was wearing a loose, long pink sweater over stretchy black pants that clung to her legs. Thick gray wool socks covered her small feet and her hair was caught up in a loosely held ponytail high on the back of her head. Silky wisps had escaped to brush against her nape. She looked sweet, young and innocent, and he wanted her so bad his teeth ached.

He needed to get this discussion over with and get out of her house before he did something he'd regret.

"Yeah," he agreed. "The kitchen is fine."

CeCe stepped past him and led the way down the hall to the kitchen, conscious of him stalking silently behind her. She paused at the table and he reached around her to pull out her chair, surrounding her for one brief moment with the scent of aftershave and warm male that was uniquely his. She steeled herself against the swift flood of heat that rushed through her veins and sat, primly folding her hands atop the table.

Zach pulled a chair away from the table and spun it around, straddling it to face her, his arms resting on the narrow edge of the wooden back. Sometime during their walk from entry hall to kitchen, he'd settled his Stetson back on his head, and his coat hung open, unbuttoned in the warmth of the house.

CeCe eyed him silently. She was damned if she was going to start this conversation.

"I shouldn't have kissed you last night," Zach said bluntly, immediately regretting his lack of finesse when her face paled, her eyes going dark with barely concealed hurt. "I've wanted to for weeks. When I found out that you didn't sleep with Aaron—'' He broke off, gesturing briefly with one hand. ''Anyway, I'm sorry.''

''Really?'' CeCe raised one eyebrow. ''I'm not. I thought it was…quite nice.''

Her frosty comment slammed into Zach, silencing him for one stunned moment. ''Nice,'' he repeated flatly, his eyes narrowing. ''You thought it was nice.''

She nodded. ''Quite nice.''

''Don't hand me that, lady.'' His voice was lethal, ominously soft. ''If that kiss was an earthquake, it would have scored a ten. Don't play games with me.''

Anger replaced CeCe's attempt to remain cool and sophisticated. ''I don't play games. And may I remind you, I wasn't the one who kissed you. *You* kissed *me*.''

''Maybe I started it,'' he said flatly. ''But you didn't exactly fight me.''

CeCe frowned. She would have loved to deny it, but he was right. ''All right, fine. What's your point?''

''My *point*,'' he said with emphasis, ''is that we generate enough heat to start a brushfire. Even Lucas noticed.''

''And you think that's bad?''

''Yes,'' he said forcefully.

CeCe eyed him speculatively. ''I thought men thought sexual heat was a good thing. Why is this bad?''

Zach glared at her. ''Because it can't go any farther, that's why.''

CeCe slowly shook her head. ''Shouldn't you wait

until I refuse to go any farther, before you assume that we will.''

''Are you telling me that if we started kissing right now like we did last night, that we absolutely, positively, wouldn't end up in your bedroom?'' he demanded.

CeCe badly wanted to lie. She hated it when he was right.

''Well, no,'' she admitted grudgingly. ''But that's not the point. Whether we would or wouldn't, you could at least ask me instead of assuming.''

Zach scrubbed a hand down his face and muttered a swearword under his breath.

''So,'' she said calmly, ''let me see if I understand you.'' She held up her hands and began to count off fingers. ''First, you've decided that you shouldn't have kissed me. Second, you've decided that it's a bad thing that we both apparently enjoyed it. Third, you've decided that we can never go beyond kissing.'' She paused and eyed him, raising one eyebrow inquiringly. ''And the third one was for what reason?''

''It's that we're bound together for years because of this ranch and that damned will. We can't have a hot affair and then go our separate ways. We're stuck with each other.'' Zach watched CeCe's eyes widen, then darken with emotion before she lowered her lashes. ''I don't see *any* woman long term,'' he said bluntly, driving his point home.

''I see.'' CeCe ignored the swift stab of pain. Her heart hurt, just as if he'd shoved a knife into her chest and buried it up to the hilt. ''Of course,'' she said, lifting her shuttered gaze to calmly meet his, "there's always the possibility that one woman might not want to see you long term. Permanent relationships, like marriage, require a great deal of commitment."

"I know," he retorted. "I've been married, and I don't ever plan to do it again."

His flat, unemotional statement startled her. CeCe couldn't read his expression. Not a muscle moved, not an eyelash flickered, not a gleam of emotion showed in his hooded eyes. "So," she said slowly, watching him carefully for reaction, "I assume that the marriage was a bad thing?"

"Yeah," he drawled, a brief, cynical smile curving his mouth. "I think you can safely assume that it wasn't a marriage made in heaven."

"Were you married a long time?"

"No."

Frustrated, CeCe frowned at him. He was being singularly uncooperative. "Getting information out of you is like pulling teeth," she told him tartly.

He stared at her for a moment before shrugging his shoulders. "It's old news—and common knowledge. I married a local girl when I was twenty-five. It lasted six months. We got divorced. I haven't seen her since. End of story."

CeCe had a feeling that there was a lot more to the story, but clearly Zach wasn't going to fill in any details.

"I see." She glanced away from him to her clasped hands and immediately loosened her clenched fingers before she purposely returned her gaze to meet his. "To return to item three," she said with commendable calm. "I have to agree that a sexual encounter might have a detrimental effect on our continued business association. Therefore, a purely platonic relationship would no doubt be in the best interests of everyone involved. I'm quite sure that it would be best for my baby."

She was so cool and businesslike that Zach wanted to shake her. Or better yet, he thought, he'd like to grab her and kiss her until all that rational composure was replaced by soft moans and heated sighs. Unfortunately, she was saying the words that agreed with his own conclusion. Still, it rankled that she would agree so easily, when reaching the decision had taken him all the long, dark hours of night.

"Right." He nodded decisively and stood, swinging the chair back to its place at the table. CeCe stood also, and walked past him to the cupboard. He breathed in air stirred gently by her passing, scented with a hint of roses and violets, and nearly groaned aloud at the willpower it took to keep from reaching for her.

"Are you going to Sarah and Josh's for Christmas dinner?"

She spoke without turning, her hands busy with wiping the countertop free of toast crumbs. Zach couldn't see her face and her voice was carefully polite.

"Yes," he said cautiously. "I am. Are you?"

"Yes, I told Sarah that I'd be there." She glanced over her shoulder, giving him a brief half smile. "And I promised her I'd bring chocolate pie."

"Well..." He shifted uneasily, eyeing her.

CeCe took pity on him. She turned to face him, crossing her arms at her waist and leaning against the counter at her back. "We're both adults, Zach, and I think you've made your point perfectly clear. We'll keep our relationship strictly platonic—no more kissing under the mistletoe, or anywhere else. Isn't that what you want?"

Zach bit back the instant denial that hovered on the tip of his tongue, and instead nodded grimly. "Yeah. That about sums it up."

"Fine." She turned away from him and swept the damp sponge across the countertop once more before tossing it into the sink. "Then we're agreed." She turned to face him again, one slender hand tucking her hair behind one ear. "We're just friends."

He couldn't read her expression, but the subtle inflection in her voice as she stressed "friends" made him uneasy. He nodded abruptly and headed for the door. "I'll see you at Sarah and Josh's."

"Right," CeCe responded. She followed him down the hall to the front door. "Bye," she called after him as he strode down the porch steps to the snowy walk.

Zach lifted his hand in farewell, but CeCe didn't watch him walk to his truck. Instead, she closed the door slowly, deliberately, and latched it, proud of herself for her self-restraint. She'd really wanted to slam it shut and scream with frustration.

"Friends. Hah!" she fumed, muttering to herself as she returned to the kitchen. "He apparently has no problem at all controlling *his* hormones."

Angus followed her into the kitchen, curling up on

the thick rug in front of the sink to eye her sympathetically. CeCe shook a wooden spoon at him.

"It's not that I *want* to get involved with him—sexually, that is. It's just these damned hormones of mine. If I weren't pregnant, I wouldn't look twice at Zach Colby."

Angus blinked at her in patent disbelief.

"Oh, all right, that's a lie," she admitted impatiently. "I'd have to be dead and in my grave not to look at him, and probably a lot more than twice. But that's not the point, Angus." She clattered pie pans on the counter and reached into the cupboard for flour. "The point is—" She stopped in midsentence and stared at Angus, her eyes unfocused. "I guess the point is, I haven't a clue how I'm going to forget that kiss under the mistletoe, not to mention the one in Jennifer's kitchen. And I'm not at all sure I've got the strength of will to resist him if he ever decides to kiss me again." She shook her head in self-disgust and turned back to the counter and the neglected pie recipe. "I hope he can resist temptation, because I doubt I can."

Christmas celebrations came and went safely and the new year arrived without mishap. Both CeCe and Zach struggled to forget the mind-blowing kiss they'd shared in Jennifer's kitchen. Neither had a great deal of success. CeCe still took Zach his morning coffee in the machine shop and dragged him into her kitchen to share lunch and conversation at noon. She was determined not to lose his help in adjusting to this new world of buttes, cold, snow and rural isolation.

Both did a fairly creditable job of convincing the other that they were coping well with their platonic relationship. Both of them were lying.

January eased slowly into February. March was due to arrive soon, but winter showed no signs of stopping. Snow piled high outside CeCe's window, and she spent long hours in front of her loom, working on a custom wall hanging for a client in Seattle. Her life had found a certain comfortable rhythm, the child in her womb growing stronger daily.

Curled up in her brass bed late one evening, Angus settled beside her, she glanced at the clock and yawned. It was after eleven and she'd been awake since six that morning.

She closed her book and stretched to set it on the nightstand. Angus grumbled complainingly at being shifted.

"Oh, hush." She smiled at the grumpy cat before switching off the lamp, throwing the bedroom into darkness. She scooted down into the bed, snuggling the covers up under her chin. "Go back to sleep, Angus."

Angus rumbled, shifted his weight to a more comfortable spot beside her feet and settled quietly. Several hours passed, the night outside growing darker and colder, before the faint cramping in her belly dragged CeCe completely awake. She pushed up on one elbow, sifting her fingers through her hair to push it out of her eyes. Shakily, she pushed back the comforter and swung her feet over the edge of the bed, waiting a moment for the room to stop swaying, before she stood and made her way to the bathroom.

"Oh, dear God." She clutched her nightgown and stared in panic at the small crimson stains against the rose-sprigged white flannel. "I'm bleeding."

She fought down the panic that threatened to overwhelm her and forced herself to think.

"I need help." One hand against the wall, one hand resting protectively over the mound of her stomach, she made her way to the kitchen and the telephone. Easing carefully onto a stool by the cabinet, she punched in the first number that came to mind and waited, heart racing, while the phone rang.

"Yeah?" The gravelly, middle-of-the-night voice was unquestionably male and blessedly familiar.

"Zach?" Her voice trembled and she bit her lip, pausing to steady herself.

"CeCe?" Surprise and growing concern chased the sleep from his deep voice. "What is it? Is something wrong?"

"I—I don't know. Yes, I think so," she managed to say. "I don't feel well. I think I should go to the hospital."

"I'll be right there. Get back in bed and stay there." Zach paused, then, "CeCe? Are you there?"

"Yes."

"Can you go back to bed?"

"Yes, I'll do that. And, Zach?"

"Yeah?"

"Hurry."

"I will, honey. I'm on my way."

Zach covered the distance from his house to the Hall ranch in record time. The house was dark, except for a light in the back. He took the steps in one long stride and didn't bother knocking, entering the house and heading down the hallway to the back bedroom.

"CeCe?" he called.

"Zach," CeCe said, sounding as if she'd never been so glad to see anyone in her life. "I'm sorry to bother you in the middle of the night like this, but I didn't know who else to call."

"Oh, hell, forget it." He shrugged off her apologies and strode across the room to her side. Her hair was fanned across the pillow, her face pale against the loose spill of dark silk. Even the lush curve of her mouth was a pale imitation of its normal rosy hue. "What is it? You're white as a ghost."

"I have stomach cramps," she told him.

His own face paled. "Is it the baby?"

"I think so."

"All right." He bent over her and caught the far edge of the comforter. He paused, one hand braced on the mattress, and looked down at her. "Is there anything you need from the house?"

"Just my purse. It has my medical card and ID in it."

"Where is it?"

CeCe glanced past him to the dresser. "There—the black leather bag on top of the dresser."

He twisted, his gaze following hers, then he stood and crossed swiftly to the dresser to collect her purse.

"This thing weighs a ton," he commented. He glanced down at her. "Can you hold it on your lap while I pick you up?"

She nodded. "Yes."

Carefully, Zach lowered the black leather bag onto her thighs, assessing the expression on her face for any pain as she took the weight. She didn't flinch. Instead, she grasped the purse to hold it in place.

"Sure it doesn't hurt?" he asked.

"Positive."

"Good. Let's get out of here."

He bent over her once again, and again CeCe breathed in the scent of cold air and the faint touch of aftershave. He caught the far edge of the rose comforter and tucked it under her, rolling her gently toward him to tuck it beneath her.

CeCe heard the harsh rasp of a deep breath and Zach froze, his hand closing tighter over her shoulder.

"What? Is something wrong?" Panic and fear clogged her voice.

"No," he reassured her swiftly. He knew the small, reddish spots that stained the back of her nightgown had to be blood. The knowledge scared the hell out of him. Maybe CeCe already knew that she was bleeding, maybe she didn't, but Zach didn't plan to be the one to tell her. There wasn't anything either of them could do about it except get her to the hospital as soon as possible. He forced himself to concentrate on getting her wrapped in the comforter. With swift, economic movements, he finished tucking the comforter snugly around her and bent, slipping his arms under her.

Cradling her securely against his chest, he strode down the hall to the front door. He had to balance her on one knee to get the door open, repeating the process outside to close the solid wooden door. The dark night was bitterly cold, with just enough wind to lift new snowfall and send it shifting along the crusted tops of snowbanks.

CeCe shivered, murmuring a soft protest as the cold wind brushed her face.

"Sorry, honey." Zach bent his head protectively, shielding her from the cold with his shoulders and the brim of his hat. "You'll be out of this wind in a minute."

Comforted, CeCe wanted to tell him she liked the sound of his deep voice calling her "honey," but she couldn't muster the energy. Instead, she curled closer, immeasurably reassured by his strength and the murmured endearment.

He'd left the truck engine running and the headlights on, warm beacons in the darkness. Once again he balanced her on one knee while he yanked open the pickup door before carefully shifting her into the warm interior of the cab. Tucking the trailing end of the thick comforter inside, he closed the door and hurried around the front of the truck to join her.

CeCe's eyes were closed, her head resting against the seat back. Zach debated for a brief moment about latching her seat belt, but decided against forcing her to sit upright for the trip into Butte Creek.

Instead, he wrapped an arm around her and lowered her sideways until her cheek rested on his jeans-covered thigh. He bent over her, lifting her legs to tuck them up onto the wide bench seat. She murmured something, and he bent lower, but couldn't understand her.

"Did I hurt you?" he asked, catching her chin in

one palm, gently turning her face toward him. Her lashes lifted and once again, he bent toward her, scanning her features.

"No, you didn't hurt me," she whispered, breathing shallowly in an effort to ride the persistent cramps that grabbed her midsection. "I'm having cramps." She was too scared to be embarrassed by the tears that welled to spill in slow, salty trails down her cheeks. "I think I might be losing my baby."

"Hey," he soothed, stroking the tears from her soft skin with his thumb. "You're not going to lose your baby. We're going to get you to the hospital and the doctor will take care of everything, so stop worrying, okay?"

CeCe badly needed to hear the words, and the utter conviction in Zach's deep voice, combined with the solid strength of his presence, reassured her as nothing else could have.

"Okay," she said shakily.

"Good." He stroked her cheek one last time, his thumb lingering to gently smooth the soft curve of her bottom lip.

"Now close your eyes and try to rest."

He shoved in the clutch and shifted the truck into gear.

CeCe closed her eyes, hearing the crunch of snow beneath the wheels as they left the ranch yard and traveled the lane to the highway. Zach turned onto the county road and the powerful engine accelerated. CeCe focused on breathing.

Zach thought the trip to Butte Creek took hours, but in reality, it was less than thirty minutes before the hospital's emergency-room lights loomed in front of him. He parked the truck in a no-parking zone, gently gathered CeCe's blanket-wrapped body and strode swiftly through the automatic doors.

The nurse on duty behind the desk jumped to her feet at the sight of Zach and his burden.

"What have we got here?" she said, scanning CeCe's face as Zach halted in front of her desk.

"She's pregnant and she's in pain. She says she has cramps," Zach said tersely.

The nurse nodded and pushed a call button on a panel as she stood and rounded the end of the metal desk. "Let's get her on a bed."

Zach followed her down a short hall and into an examining room. The nurse dropped the railing on a narrow bed and helped unwrap CeCe from the rose comforter so Zach could lower her onto the white sheet. Relieved though he was at knowing CeCe would have a doctor's care, still his arms were reluctant to release her.

"Are you the husband?" the nurse asked.

Her words didn't register. Zach stood at CeCe's bedside, her small hand enclosed in his, studying the pale, drawn lines of her face and the dark lashes that lay like sable fans against delicate skin.

"Sir? Sir?"

The nurse's repeated request finally got his attention and he glanced up to find her watching him.

"I'm sorry—what did you say?"

The nurse smiled understandingly. "I asked if you're her husband."

Zach shook his head. "No—no, I'm not. She's a

widow. I'm her neighbor." The depth of his regret that it was so surprised him. Did he want to be her husband? He shoved the thought aside, focusing on the nurse.

"I'll have to ask you to step out while I check her. I rang upstairs for the doctor. He should be here any moment. If you'll have a seat by my desk, I'll have some forms to fill out."

"Yeah, fine." Zach squeezed CeCe's hand reassuringly and was rewarded by a flicker of her lashes. He bent low, his lips brushing against the delicate shell of her ear as he spoke. "I'll be right outside if you want me, honey. The nurse is here and the doctor's on his way."

"You aren't leaving?" Her lashes lifted, the soft gray eyes reflecting swift panic.

"No," he said quietly. "I'll be right outside in the waiting room."

"Okay," she whispered, a brief curve of her lips registering relief.

Zach squeezed her hand once more and stepped back, leaving her to the ministrations of the nurse. As he reached the hall, he nearly collided with a white-coated doctor. The rumpled condition of the man's hair gave mute testimony that he'd been pulled from his bed by the emergency-room buzzer.

Zach nodded in greeting and held the door open, receiving a brief nod in return before the doctor disappeared into the room.

Zach returned to the nurses' station but didn't sit down. He paced back and forth between the outside doors and the hallway that led to the room where

CeCe lay, growing steadily more impatient and uneasy.

At last, the door opened and the doctor stepped into the hallway. He looked up, saw Zach, and immediately walked toward him.

"You brought Ms. Hawkins in?" he asked.

"Yes." Zach nodded.

"I'm going to admit her. Is there family that needs to be notified?"

Zach's heart jumped into his throat. "Is she going to lose the baby?"

Chapter Eight

"**I** hope not. We're going to do everything we can to make sure she doesn't." The doctor scanned Zach's face and held out his hand. "I'm Dr. Spurling. Nurse Tompkins told me Mrs. Hawkins is a widow. Are you a family member?"

"No," Zach said tersely, clasping the doctor's palm in a brief handshake. "I'm her neighbor. She doesn't have any family in the area. Her parents live in Seattle."

"I see." The doctor nodded. "I'll ask her if she wants them notified."

Behind them, the elevator pinged to announce its arrival and the doors whooshed open to disclose a white-uniformed nurse.

"The patient's in room 101," Dr. Spurling called.

The nurse nodded and disappeared into the examination room and the doctor turned back to Zach.

"We're going to take Ms. Hawkins up to the second floor, room 212, and get her settled in. Give the nurses about fifteen to twenty minutes to make her comfortable and then you can see her if you want."

"Fine." Zach laid a hand on the doctor's forearm as he moved to turn away down the hall. "What exactly is wrong? Is she in any danger?"

"Not at the moment. But she's losing blood—not a lot, but enough to give us some concern. We're going to put her on medication to stop the bleeding and the cramping and keep her in the hospital so we can monitor her closely."

Zach felt a rush of relief. "So CeCe's life isn't in danger. What about the baby?"

"If the medication doesn't stop the bleeding and cramping, then the fetus could be endangered. But I have no reason to believe that the medication won't work," the doctor reassured him. "Ms. Hawkins is very healthy, and the baby is strong—both are important factors."

"I see." Zach nodded.

The doctor smiled and gave Zach's shoulder a brief, comforting pat. "I have every reason to believe that I'll be sending her home in a few days."

"Good," Zach said with feeling.

The exam-room door opened and the two nurses wheeled a gurney into the hall, CeCe's pregnant form under the white sheet and blanket.

Dr. Spurling gestured down the hall toward the front of the hospital. "Nurse Tompkins told me that there's a fresh pot of coffee downstairs in the cafeteria. She made it just before you arrived with Ms. Hawkins. Help yourself and come on upstairs. By the time you get there, the nurses should be nearly finished settling our patient.''

''Thanks, Doc.'' Zach shook the doctor's hand and watched him enter the elevator with the two nurses and the gurney that held CeCe before he headed down the hallway. His eyes felt as if they had a pound of sand in each one. He hoped caffeine would scrub the gritty feeling from his eyes and wipe the cobwebs from his brain.

The coffee helped a lot. So did the cold water that he splashed on his face in the bathroom before he headed up the stairwell to the second floor.

CeCe came awake slowly. Muted voices and the faint sounds of human activity sifted through the layers of sleep that cushioned her, tugging her closer to wakefulness.

Why are people in my house?

She frowned, aware that she should know the answer to the question, but the correct response was elusive, floating just out of her reach. She shifted her legs and missed Angus's warm, heavy weight against her feet. Her frown deepened and she forced her heavy eyelids upward.

This isn't my bedroom. The startling discovery gave way to memory and her hands flew to her midsection.

Thank God. The burgeoning swell of her belly was blessedly familiar and she drew in a deep, shaky breath, opening her eyes fully to survey the room. Her gaze swept slowly over the white wall unit with its cabinets and sink, and a wide door that she guessed led to the hallway. She turned her head against the crisp white pillow, her eyes widening as she found Zach.

He was slouched in an armchair beside her bed, his head propped against the chair back at an angle she thought surely must guarantee cramped muscles. His jaw was shadowed and rough with beard stubble, his hair tousled. The chair was much too small for his tall, broad frame, and he sat with one leg bent at the knee, the other stretched out in front of him.

He looked exhausted and wonderfully, solidly dear. CeCe considered waking him, but indulged instead in the rare opportunity to study him unnoticed.

"Good morning." The nurse's cheerful greeting accompanied the unexpected opening of the door.

Zach's eyes shot open and he stared straight into CeCe's. She couldn't look away; she didn't even try. She wasn't sure what he read in her gaze, but his blue gaze darkened before he glanced at the approaching nurse and quickly shoved upright, shifting his boots out of her path.

"Good morning," CeCe answered, compelled to stop staring at Zach when the nurse stepped between them, catching CeCe's wrist in her hand. The white-uniformed RN quickly placed her fingers over the pulse beat and focused on her watch.

"How are we feeling this morning?" she asked briskly, never taking her gaze from her wristwatch.

"Much better than last night," CeCe answered promptly.

"Good." The nurse popped a thermometer in CeCe's mouth with swift efficiency. "Hold that under your tongue."

"Yes, ma'am," CeCe mumbled.

The nurse turned and smiled at Zach, her brown eyes twinkling in her round face. "I declare, Zachariah, I haven't seen you in ages."

Zach shrugged and shifted uncomfortably. "The hospital is a place I try to stay away from, Mary Lou."

"Well, I can understand that," the nurse agreed. She glanced at her watch and turned back to CeCe, slipping the thermometer out to peer intently at the reading. She jotted a note on the chart at the end of the bed. "I'm going to chase you out of here, Zach. It's time for Ms. Hawkins to visit the bathroom before we serve breakfast, and that cute little designer hospital gown she's wearing wasn't made for privacy."

Zach stood, groaning silently as his bones and muscles protested their being cramped in the uncomfortable chair for too many long hours. He glanced around, found his hat and jacket draped over the seat of a metal chair and swept them up, settling the Stetson on his head and slinging his jacket over one shoulder before he turned back to CeCe. She looked much too fragile, surrounded as she was by the clinical paraphernalia of the hospital room.

"I have to go home and feed the stock," he told her. "Do you need anything from your house? I can swing by there on my way back."

Relief that he was returning swept CeCe. "Not that I can think of," she said. "But thanks."

"No problem." The soft smile she gave him rocked Zach. He didn't want to leave her. The urge to stay was so strong that he felt compelled to deny the need. He nodded abruptly and left the room.

"I understand Zach brought you in to emergency last night?" the nurse asked.

CeCe forced herself to stop thinking about Zach and focus on the nurse. "Yes, he did."

"Hmm." The nurse shifted the bed railing, sliding it down, before she adjusted the bed, raising the head with the remote-control button until CeCe was almost sitting up. "Let's get you out of bed, dearie."

She helped CeCe swing her legs over the edge of the bed. "You caused quite a stir in the nurses' lounge this morning."

CeCe paused, glancing curiously at the chatty woman. "I did? Why?"

"Because Zach Colby carried you into the emergency room before dawn and then refused to leave your bedside." Nurse Mary Lou winked at CeCe, her round face wreathed in an impish grin. "Half of the single women in the county would walk barefoot over hot coals just to get him to notice them and say hello, let alone what you accomplished. Of course, none of them has a chance."

"Oh." CeCe wasn't surprised that other women noticed the handsome rancher, but she didn't like the twinge of unmistakable green jealousy the statement caused. Still, she couldn't resist asking the obvious question. "Why don't they have a chance?"

"Ever since he divorced that wife of his, it's plain as the nose on your face that young man has absolutely no use for women." The nurse slipped hospital-issue slippers on CeCe's feet and caught her arm to help her stand up.

"He must have loved her a lot," CeCe said neutrally.

"Loved her?" the nurse snorted disbelievingly. "Hardly. He did the right thing by her and then found out that she'd lied through her teeth."

Puzzled, CeCe halted and stared at the gossipy woman. "Excuse me? I don't understand."

"His wife—she lied to him." Nurse Mary Lou urged CeCe forward. "Told him she was pregnant so he'd marry her, then he found out there wasn't a baby and never had been. Oldest trick in the book, my husband says, but you wouldn't think it would have caught Zach. He didn't waste any time getting rid of her, though. They were divorced six months after they were married."

CeCe was stunned, but before she could ask even one of the burning questions that sprang to mind, the nurse hustled her into the bathroom and whisked out of the room, closing the door behind her. Left alone, CeCe stood perfectly still, staring into the mirror at her reflection.

I know Zach told me his marriage wasn't good, she thought, *but it sounds as if it was a disaster. No wonder he has a low opinion of women—with the exception of Sarah and Jennifer.*

"Breakfast is here," Mary Lou called through the closed door.

"I'll be right out." CeCe hastily turned on the tap and bent over the sink.

She didn't get an opportunity to further quiz the busybody nurse about Zach's marriage and divorce, even though her stay in the hospital slipped into two days, then three. When the Hightowers crowded into the room to visit, she didn't have a chance to query Jennifer or Sarah without Lucas or Josh hearing. And she didn't want either man to tell Zach she was curious about his ex-wife.

Dr. Spurling turned her case over to her regular doctor, and on the fourth morning, she greeted Dr. Johnson with a militant gleam in her eye.

"I want to go home," she said firmly.

"I know. You told me yesterday. And the day before," he responded, his faded blue eyes twinkling behind wire-framed glasses. "And my answer is the same. I want you to have complete bed rest, and if I keep you in the hospital, I'm sure you'll get it."

"I can rest just as well at home as here," CeCe insisted. "Probably better, since lying in this bed with nothing to do is driving me crazy."

"But that's exactly the point," Dr. Johnson said firmly. "*Nothing* is precisely what I want you to do. Absolutely nothing but rest."

"I can rest at home," she repeated stubbornly. "But there I'll be in my own comfortable bed with my books to read, a pot of tea and my cat to curl up beside me for company."

"And who's going to brew the pot of tea for you? And feed the cat?"

"I will."

The deep, masculine voice interrupted them. Startled, both CeCe and Dr. Johnson turned to stare at the doorway. Zach stood just inside the room, his heavy coat unbuttoned and hanging open, his hands tucked into the deep pockets, his Stetson pushed back on his head.

"You will?" Dr. Johnson asked with interest.

"No, he won't," CeCe said just as promptly.

"Sure I will." The heated exchange between CeCe and her doctor had blocked the sounds of the opening door and Zach had heard most of their conversation. He hated hospitals and thought he knew exactly how CeCe felt about staying here. If CeCe wanted out, he'd take her home with him. The doc said that all she needed was rest. "I've been feeding your cat for the last three days and how hard can it be to pour hot water over tea leaves? You'll stay at my place until the doc says you can go home."

"Oh no I won't." CeCe glared at him. "I'm going *home*, to my home. Not yours. I want my own bed, and my own teapot, in my own house."

"You can't go home alone," Dr. Johnson repeated firmly, fixing her with an implacable stare.

"I promise I'll rest and not work," CeCe said. "I would never do anything to risk losing my baby."

"I know you wouldn't," Dr. Johnson conceded. "But I want you off your feet for at least two weeks. That means no cooking meals, no puttering around the kitchen to brew tea and feed the cat, no running your bath, no loading clothes in the washer—the list is endless. And everything on the list is something that, like most women, you probably do on automatic pilot and don't think twice about.''

CeCe's fingers twisted in the white sheet. ''I suppose you're right,'' she admitted reluctantly. ''But now that you've brought it to my attention, I promise I'll let dust sit on the furniture and let the laundry overflow in the hamper.''

''What about feeding the cat?'' Zach asked. ''Not to mention feeding you?''

CeCe frowned at him. ''I'll stack cans of cat food and a can opener at the foot of my bed and have pizza delivered every night.''

Amusement lit Zach's blue eyes.

''Well, the cat food might work,'' he drawled. ''But you can't get pizza delivered to your house—this isn't Seattle, sweetheart.''

CeCe's frown deepened into a threatening glare. Unfortunately, he was right, she fumed.

Zach watched her anger fade to resignation, her bottom lip trembling before she firmed her chin, sniffed disparagingly and pointedly looked away from him to the doctor.

''It seems this is a stalemate,'' she admitted. ''Apparently I have no alternative to the hospital.''

''Well, actually…'' Dr. Johnson's keen gaze skipped from CeCe's dejected face to Zach and back again. ''I think there is a possible solution.''

''There is? What?''

''If you weren't alone at your house, if someone was willing to stay with you and make sure that you stayed in bed and rested, I could let you go home.''

CeCe's gaze raced from the doctor's face to Zach. The abrupt silence was fraught with tension.

"I suppose I could stay at your house, instead of taking you to mine, since you're too stubborn to be practical and come home with me," Zach said.

CeCe had an instant image of Zach living in her house with her—sharing the bathroom, sharing the long winter evenings…sharing her bed? She swiftly shook her head.

"No. That's impossible. You can't stay with me."

"Sure I can. The house is half mine."

CeCe's mouth dropped open before her eyes narrowed challengingly and she snapped her lips closed so fast that she heard her teeth click in protest. "That's not true. Is it?"

"Sure it is. The will says the ranch is split fifty-fifty. It doesn't specify who gets the house, so I figure half the house is mine. I'll stay in my half—you stay in yours. It shouldn't be that hard, should it?"

CeCe bit her tongue to keep from using a swearword that would have shocked her mother. *If he can take it, so can I,* she told herself grimly.

She turned to Dr. Johnson. "Are you truly convinced that if I go home alone, performing simple daily tasks might endanger the baby?"

"I am."

CeCe sighed and gave in. "Then it seems that I have no option but to accept your offer, Zach. If you would kindly approve my release, Dr. Johnson, I'll be leaving."

The doctor smiled with satisfaction, his eyes twinkling with amusement, and sketched her a brief bow.

"I'll take care of the necessary papers immediately."
He turned, the tail of his white lab coat swirling as
he headed for the door. His back to CeCe, he clapped
a hand on Zach's shoulder and winked conspiratori-
ally before whisking briskly through the door.

Zach assessed CeCe's narrow-eyed stare and decided retreat was the wisest choice. "I'll bring the
truck around to the entrance," he told her. He lifted
his hat, settled it over his forehead, and left the room.

CeCe stared at the closed door. "What have I
done?" she murmured aloud. "I'm not sure that I can
live in the same house with Zach. Maybe he can turn
attraction on and off at will, but I can't." *But he
spends most of his days away from the house working,*
she reminded herself. *I probably won't see him at all
except for a few moments in the morning and in the
evenings.*

The only alternative was to remain in the hospital—an option CeCe was willing to do almost anything to avoid.

Zach wasn't sure that CeCe wouldn't change her
mind until a nurse pushed her wheelchair off the elevator and down the main hall toward the front entrance. He shoved away from the wall he leaned
against and followed them outside.

The winter sunshine did little to warm the cold air,
but CeCe tipped her face up anyway, obviously rel-
ishing the fresh, crisp air.

"I feel like I've been cooped up in that hospital
room forever." She sighed.

The nurse chuckled. "Nice to get outside, isn't it?"

"Definitely," CeCe agreed wholeheartedly.

"Here we are," Zach said. The nurse halted the wheelchair next to Zach's pickup, locking the brakes and stepping in front of CeCe to flip up the footrests.

"I'll do the rest." Zach bent and lifted CeCe into his arms, settling her easily onto the bench seat in the truck cab.

CeCe called a swift goodbye to the friendly nurse just before Zach closed the door, shutting her inside the cab. He touched the brim of his hat in farewell and rounded the front of the pickup. The nurse waved and smiled at CeCe, then turned away and went up the sidewalk toward the front entrance as he pulled open the truck door and slid beneath the steering wheel.

The cab's interior was comfortably heated; in the few moments before the door closed, his entry let in a breath of frigid winter air. He turned toward CeCe and leaned closer to check the latch on her seat belt. Satisfied that it was secure, he sat back and searched her face.

"Are you comfortable?"

"Yes, thank you."

"Warm enough?"

"Yes, thank you." He was half-turned toward her, one arm resting along the curve of the steering wheel, the other along the back of the seat. CeCe was much too aware of him, his body nearly bracketing hers within the warm confines of the cab. She was more intimidated, however, by the concern in his normally cool eyes. It was easier to deal with him when they were arguing. At least then she didn't have this urge to lean forward and wrap her arms around him. "And thank you for volunteering to save me from the hospital."

"No problem." Zach smiled at her. "I've been stuck in the hospital a time or two and I hated every minute."

"Really?"

"Yeah. A green-broke horse threw me and I broke my leg once. I was in a cast for several weeks. It was like being sentenced to jail time."

CeCe nodded, convinced that he understood. "It seems like such a waste of time. There are a dozen things I could be doing at home. Even if I stay in bed," she said hastily when he frowned at her. His forehead cleared and she shifted on the seat. "Anyway, I'm very appreciative of your offer and I'll try not to cause you too much trouble."

A grin broke over Zach's face. "CeCe, the day you don't cause trouble will be the day hell freezes over."

"What do you mean?" she demanded.

"Just what I said." He chucked her under the chin and her eyes snapped at him, her hand swatting quickly at his. "All women are trouble—some one kind, some another. And some more than others," he added as he turned back to the steering wheel and shifted the truck into gear.

"Hmmph," CeCe sniffed, crossing her arms over her chest. "That's a sexist comment if I ever heard one."

She was rewarded by a deep chuckle. Swiftly she glanced sideways at him, but he was in profile while he drove, the strong lines of his face eased with laughter. She sighed silently and returned her own gaze to the snowy road ahead. He was always a threat to her equilibrium, but when he was relaxed, treating her with comfortable friendliness, he was doubly dangerous. She sighed again, resigned to being tortured for the next two weeks.

Zach parked in front of her gate and switched off the engine.

"Don't move," he warned her before he stepped out of the cab and rounded the hood to pull open her door. He slipped an arm around her waist, the other under her knees, and swung her out of the truck, elbowing the door shut behind them. Snow crunched under his boots as he strode up the walk to the front porch.

"Did it snow last night?" CeCe asked, busily assessing the familiar house and yard, pleased with the satisfying sense of homecoming.

"Yes, maybe an inch or two," Zach replied. He reached the front door and glanced down at her. "Can you open the door?"

CeCe turned the knob and pushed. The door swung inward, aided by Zach's shoulder applied to its heavy wood.

"Home sweet home," she murmured, smiling with delight.

Zach glanced down at the woman in his arms. Her face glowed with pleasure and he felt a surge of satisfaction that she was so obviously happy. He strode down the hall and was immediately attacked by Angus.

"Meow!" The huge cat rubbed against Zach's leg,

his greeting growing steadily louder and more demanding.

"Angus." CeCe reached her hand toward him and the cat jumped to reach her, sniffing at her fingertips, his sandpaper-rough tongue brushing a brief, raspy welcome across her palm.

Zach carried CeCe into her bedroom and lowered her onto the bed. Angus immediately leaped up beside her, purring with delight and rubbing against her hand in a demand for attention. CeCe laughed and scratched him between the ears.

"I think he's glad to see me."

The orange-and-white-striped cat climbed onto her lap, rubbing his head beneath her chin and purring loudly while he rhythmically kneaded his claws against her wool jacket. CeCe hugged him, smoothing her cheek against the warmth of his sleek, thick fur.

Zach snapped on the bedside lamp and turned back to watch her hug, pet and croon to the tomcat. *I know exactly how he feels,* he thought with self-derision as he watched the cat revel in her attention. *Only I'd much rather have her sit on my lap while she petted me.*

"...much better, don't you think?"

Zach realized that CeCe was speaking to him, but he had no idea what she'd asked him.

"Sorry, I didn't hear you. Don't I think what?"

CeCe gave him a quizzical look. "I said that being home is much better than being confined in the hospital and I asked if you agreed."

"Oh. Yeah, right." Zach glanced consideringly around the bedroom, hands on hips, before his gaze

returned to her. She still wore her green jacket over
the sweater and jeans he'd brought to the hospital for
her. She'd unbuttoned it while they were talking and
Angus was curled on her lap, humming contentedly.
''I guess I should get you out of that coat and put on
the teakettle.'' He glanced at Angus. ''I've already
fed the cat. I stopped in this morning before I came
to the hospital.''

CeCe shifted Angus off her lap and onto the woven
blue blanket. Before she could shrug out of her coat,
Zach leaned over the bed and tugged one sleeve free.
He slipped an arm around her shoulders and reached
around her to slide the jacket off.

''I can get it.'' CeCe's words were muffled against
his shirtfront. She breathed in the heady scent of aftershave, crisp cotton and the subtle male scent that
was Zach and unconsciously pressed closer.

He removed her jacket and stood, the dark green
wool coat dangling from his fingers. ''Already done.''
He scanned her sweater and jeans, tossed the jacket
down at the foot of the bed and picked up her foot,
swiftly untying her bootlaces.

''Hey! What are you doing?'' she protested.

''Taking off your boots.'' He glanced down at her,
his blue gaze carrying a warning. ''You're not getting
out of bed, so you don't need them.''

''Oh.'' CeCe acquiesced, bracing herself against
the mattress and watching him while he pulled off her
boot with efficient ease and picked up her other foot.

He dealt with the second set of laces just as swiftly
before he set the boots neatly beside her bed. His gaze
ran swiftly upward from her wool socks, over her

jeans and sweater to her eyes, then reversed the trip
with much less speed before stroking with slow thor-
oughness back up her body to find her gray eyes once
again.

CeCe saw the speculative gleam in his eyes and
held up a hand, palm out. "No." she said firmly.

Zach smiled at her, a slow, lethal smile that both
threatened and promised. He'd never looked at her
quite like that before and CeCe sucked in her breath,
suddenly vividly aware of the waning afternoon light
outside and the intimacy created by the pool of lamplight in the soft, early twilight that filled her bedroom.

"No?" he drawled, one eyebrow lifting in inquiry.

"No," she repeated. "There's a limit to what I
need help removing, Zach. You've reached it."

"Dr. Johnson specifically said you're not to exert
yourself," he reminded her, his deep voice warm and
slow as molasses.

"True. And if you start removing anything else,
I'll have to exert myself and assault you."

He threw back his head and laughed. CeCe loved
the sound. She loved what happened to his face when
he laughed. The stern lines relaxed, and he looked
young and carefree.

His laughter subsided to a grin that continued to
tug at the corners of his mouth. "All right, I'll go put
the teakettle on."

"Good plan," she said dryly. She scooted to the
head of the bed and stacked the pillows, tucking them
behind her. Propped against the brass headboard, she
watched him pick up a woven throw from the dressing table's old-fashioned, low bench seat. He shook

it out, letting it settle over her feet and legs, and tucked it loosely around her waist. "Thank you."

"You're welcome."

He stayed where he was, his arms braced on either side of her, and contemplated her expression. He glanced at the bedside table's clock, then back at CeCe.

"It's nearly four o'clock. If I make you a pot of tea and something to snack on, will you promise to behave yourself and stay in bed while I feed the stock?"

"Yes. I promise."

"Good." He stood and headed for the door.

"You're enjoying this, aren't you?" she accused with mild irritation.

Zach turned back, one eyebrow quirking upward. "What?"

"This." CeCe spread her hands to indicate herself, the bed and the room. "You love giving orders and now I have to listen. You have a legitimate excuse to browbeat me."

"I'm not browbeating you," he denied. "I'm just doing what I promised Doc Johnson I'd do—keeping you in bed."

CeCe's gaze sharpened over his features, but his face remained blandly innocent. "You can stop worrying about enforcing the doctor's restrictions," she said. "I'm not going to do anything that might harm my baby."

His gaze followed her hand as it smoothed comfortingly over the soft blue wool covering her midsection. He had to admit that she was obsessively protective of the child she carried beneath her heart. "That's a lucky kid you've got there, CeCe Hawkins," he said softly. "I'll be right back with your tea."

CeCe stared at the empty doorway. For a moment, Zach had stared at her as if he was baffled and bemused. She wasn't sure exactly what she'd done to bring that soft smile to his face, but wished she could do it again. She picked up Angus and cuddled him close, rubbing her face against his warm, soft fur and taking comfort in the simple, uncomplicated affection he gave her so willingly.

Two hours later, CeCe heard the front door open and close.

"CeCe, it's me."

She closed the book she'd been reading and gazed expectantly at the doorway. Tipping her head to listen, she cataloged the sounds he made and guessed that Zach was shedding his heavy coat, hat and boots in the entryway. Moments later, he filled her doorway.

"Hi." She hadn't heard his footsteps as he approached down the hallway because he wore thick socks.

"Hi," he responded. He glanced at the wooden tea tray beside her on the bed and lifted an eyebrow. "Did you stay in bed?"

"Yes. I did." CeCe gestured to the duffel bag he carried. "Two of the bedrooms upstairs are guest rooms. Pick whichever one you want to use. The other two I've been cleaning and painting for a nursery and master bedroom."

Zach's gaze ran over the warm, comfortable interior of the bedroom. "You're moving out of this room?"

CeCe's glance traveled around the room, lingering on the view outside the window. "Not until early summer. I'll keep the baby here with me in a bassinet when she's newborn, then we'll move upstairs and she can have a room of her own with me in the bedroom next door."

"Oh. I see." He also saw that CeCe Hawkins was perfectly happy planning a life that included only her and her child. For some reason, that bothered him. He hefted the duffel bag. "I'll drop this upstairs and start dinner. Are you hungry?"

CeCe smiled ruefully. "I'm always hungry. How about you?"

"I could eat." He nodded in agreement. "Annabel, Jennifer and Sarah came by last night and filled the freezer. We won't starve, that's for sure. I'll be back."

Dinner was surprisingly good. CeCe hadn't any preconceived notions about what kind of a cook Zach might be, since they'd never discussed the subject.

He carried away the tray and she heard water running in the kitchen, followed by the clatter of crockery. She returned to the mystery novel she'd been reading before dinner and struggled to immerse herself in the story once more. The author was one of her favorites, but CeCe just couldn't stay interested. She stared absentmindedly at the same page she'd read two times in the last fifteen minutes, and realized that she would have to read it once more, because she wasn't sure whose corpse had just washed up on the Los Angeles beach.

Zach leaned against the doorjamb, watching CeCe. Her slim fingers twisted a strand of hair between thumb and forefinger and her mouth had a disconsolate, downward curve.

"Hey," he called softly. His voice clearly startled her, for she jumped, and her gaze flew to his face. "What's wrong?"

"Nothing. I'm fine."

"No, you're not," he disagreed. "I can tell by the look on your face." His glance dropped to the book she'd lowered facedown over her midriff. "You're not still worried about the baby, are you?"

CeCe sighed, her fingers tightening over the edges of the book. "Maybe a little."

"Don't. Doc Johnson assured me there's no reason to believe that you'll have further problems—not as long as you do exactly as he told you and get plenty of rest."

"I'm sure he's right." CeCe gave him a wry smile. "Have I told you that I'm a chronic worrier?"

Zach nodded. "I think you mentioned it a time or two. And I've noticed that you have a tendency to obsess."

"I do not obsess," CeCe said firmly.

"No?" Zach cocked an eyebrow in patent disbelief. "What would you call it?"

"Serious focusing," she answered promptly.

He looked at her and shook his head. "And you

actually said that with a straight face. I'm impressed.''

CeCe bit back a smile and shrugged. "All right. I'll admit to having a teensy problem with overfocusing on occasion.''

Zach rolled his eyes and snorted.

CeCe laughed outright. "You're not going to get me to admit that you're right," she told him. "You're already going to be impossible because you think you're in control here.''

Her gray eyes sparkled, her face lit with amusement. For the moment, he'd distracted her from worrying about her baby's health. Zach grinned at her with satisfaction and started across the room. "I don't just think I'm in control, I know I am. Doc Johnson said so, and don't you forget it.''

Before CeCe could respond, he took the book from her and set it on the bedside table. Then he slipped one arm around her waist, the other under her knees, and picked her up, blanket and all.

"What are you doing?'' CeCe demanded.

"Taking you out into the living room,'' he responded calmly. "You need a change of scenery and I feel like watching a movie.''

Chapter Nine

Diverted, CeCe tried to ignore the messages her nerve endings were sending her and concentrate on his words.

"What kind of a movie?" she asked with interest.

"What kind have you got?" he asked, turning sideways to maneuver them through the bedroom doorway and into the hall.

"Dramas, comedies, musicals, westerns—but no horror. I can't watch gory terror."

"Too bad. I had my heart set on watching a creature from outer space eat humans."

"That's disgusting."

Zach glanced down at her pursed lips and wrinkled nose and chuckled. "Everybody's a critic. I suppose this means that you don't read Stephen King novels, either?"

"Sometimes," CeCe responded as he settled her on the sofa. He grabbed her ankles and gently swung her legs up on the seat cushions. "I like some of his short stories. And I read Dean Koontz on occasion."

Zach switched on the television but the screen held only static. He picked up the remote, turned down the sound and changed channels, but the reception was the same.

"Have you been having problems with reception?" he asked, glancing over his shoulder at CeCe.

"Always," she said dryly.

Hands on hips, he turned to look at her. "What do you mean, 'always'? Did you report it to the satellite company?"

"I would have if I had a satellite dish, but since I don't have one, I didn't report it."

"You don't have a satellite dish?" Zach stared at her in disbelief. "Then you don't have TV reception."

"Only rarely—and with a lot of interference."

Zach frowned. "Why not?"

"Why not what?"

"Why don't you have a satellite dish?"

"It's not in my budget."

His frown turned into a glare. "I thought you told me that you didn't need money?"

CeCe frowned back at him. "I don't."

"If you can't afford a satellite dish, then you need money," he said bluntly.

"That's your opinion," she said stubbornly. "But it's not mine."

"That's the opinion of any reasonable adult," he

argued. "You can't even get the evening news, for God's sake."

"Yes, I can. I have a great FM radio with a twenty-four-hour news station."

"Well, satellite television has twenty-four-hour news stations, too. Not to mention movie channels."

Amusement flashed in her gray eyes. "Ah, but they probably run horror films, which I wouldn't want to watch anyway."

A reluctant grin tilted Zach's mouth. "Maybe. But think about all the other movies you're missing."

CeCe smiled. "True." She sobered. "I live on a budget, Zach. I always have, but with the extra expense of getting ready for Baby, I don't have room in my budget for the cost of a satellite dish. That doesn't mean I'm poverty-stricken or deprived, it just means that I had to make a choice and I chose to do without television for a while."

Zach didn't want her to have to make choices and do without anything. He shrugged away the urge to tell her so and looked at the television screen where video snow was accompanied by muted audio static. He looked back at her. "If you don't have television reception, what did you mean when you told me you have movies?"

"I collect videos of my favorite movies. It's a hobby." She gestured toward the cabinet below the television. "Open the doors."

Zach dropped onto his heels in front of the cabinet and pulled open the doors. Inside was a state-of-the-art VCR and dozens of videotapes. He ran a forefinger over the spines of several tape cases and whistled.

The shelves held an eclectic collection of classics along with newer contemporary films. "You weren't kidding when you said you had movies. What do you want to watch?"

"You pick one. I've seen them all, but I watch them over and over."

Zach selected a tape, inserted it in the VCR and retreated to the sofa to join CeCe. Without asking, he casually picked up her ankles and dropped onto the cushions, stretching out comfortably with her feet cradled on his lap.

Bemused, CeCe stared at him. He'd settled into her life and home as easily as if they'd done this a million times before. She wondered fleetingly how many other women he'd shared housing with to be this relaxed with the situation. However, given his declared avoidance of women, she decided, this surely couldn't be a frequent occurrence for him.

He held the remote control out in front of him and thumbed the play switch. The tape began to run and CeCe's attention was caught by the ominous roll of drums and thunderous crash of cymbals. She looked away from Zach just in time to see the title of an action-adventure movie starring one of her favorite actors scroll across the screen.

"I should have known you'd pick a guy flick."

"A guy flick?" Zach rolled his head sideways against the back of the sofa and eyed her. "This is from your movie collection, remember."

"True." CeCe grinned and settled back against the pillows. "And I love the part where the hero single-handedly takes on a barroom full of twenty guys and annihilates all of them."

"You would," Zach said dryly. "I'm just surprised that it's not the heroine that wipes out a crowded barroom."

"That's in another movie," she told him pointedly.

"Ah. I knew there had to be one somewhere." He faced front and focused his attention on the movie.

The movie and good-natured wrangling accomplished just what Zach had hoped. CeCe forgot to worry about the baby. When the movie ended, she yawned, glanced at her watch and gasped.

"My goodness. Look at the time. I didn't realize it was so late."

"Why do you care?" Zach asked lazily, absentmindedly rubbing her feet. Encased in wool socks and covered by the blanket, they were still small-boned and delicate. "It's not like you have to be up early tomorrow."

"I wasn't thinking about me. I was thinking about you."

Zach shrugged. "Don't worry about me. I have to get up early and feed the stock, but if I'm tired, I can always go back to bed when I'm done."

"Yes, but do you ever actually go back to bed after you're up and out?" CeCe asked skeptically.

"Not often." He gave her a lazy smile. "The good news is, I'm my own boss. The bad news is, I'm my own boss. I don't punch a time clock, work is never finished and there's always one more job waiting to be done, but if I want to take time off, I do."

"It must be nice," CeCe said reflectively. "That

sort of independence is what I'm hoping to develop with my weaving. I love setting my own work schedule, but I have to confess I'm not as happy with the lack of predictability and slow growth I've seen.''

''Have you had any problems working so far from your market?'' Zach asked curiously.

''Actually, very few. I originally thought that living so far from Seattle might present a problem, but up to now, I haven't found any obstacles that I couldn't get past with my fax machine or the good old United States Postal Service.''

''Good.''

The movie credits ended and noisy tape static rose in volume. Zach grabbed the remote control and ejected the tape before he clicked off the television and VCR. He shifted CeCe's feet and legs onto the sofa and stood, bending over to swing her up into his arms once more.

This time, she looped her arms around his neck.

''Are you going to do this every time I move from one room to another?'' she asked conversationally.

''Sure. Why?''

''Oh, no reason. I just wondered.''

Zach halted outside the bathroom door, nudging it farther open with his foot. Still holding CeCe, he looked down at her. ''Need any help?'' he offered.

She gave him a direct look. ''No.''

''Too bad.'' He released her, setting her on her feet. ''Call me when you're finished,'' he told her firmly.

''Yes, sir,'' she said sweetly. She planted her palm against the blue plaid flannel shirt covering his broad chest and pushed. He gave way, backing out of the bathroom, and she closed the door firmly, shutting him out.

Zach crossed his arms over his chest and leaned against the opposite wall, prepared to wait until she opened the door again. He doubted that she'd obey his command and call him. The bedroom was only a few feet down the hall, but he was damned if he was going to give up the chance to hold her again.

I could get used to this, he thought. After only one afternoon and evening of living in the same house with CeCe Hawkins, he was already trying to think of ways to prolong the living arrangement. *Face it, Colby,* he thought derisively, *now that you're sleeping under her roof, you want her to invite you into her bed. Pregnant or not, regardless of whose baby she's carrying, you want her. Period. In spite of all your talk about "just friends."* He wondered briefly how many cold showers he'd have to take while he waited for her to recover, physically and emotionally, from the trauma of the last few days.

CeCe pulled the bathroom door open and stopped in midstep. Zach leaned against the opposite wall, arms crossed, an unreadable expression on his face. He lifted one eyebrow and eyed her silently.

"I don't need to be carried," she said, returning his stare. "My bedroom is only a few feet down the hall."

"Dr. Johnson said you were to have complete bed rest," Zach said implacably as he pushed away from the wall. He bent and swung her up against his chest. "He didn't say it was all right to walk a few feet."

CeCe muttered something unintelligible.

"What's that?" Zach glanced down at her and found her gray eyes threatening retribution.

"Never mind," she said tartly.

Zach carried her into her bedroom and set her on the bed.

"You are not staying in here while I get ready for bed," she told him firmly.

"Of course not," he said calmly. "Can you get ready for bed without standing up?"

"Why?" She narrowed her eyes at him suspiciously.

"Because if you can't, I'm staying."

CeCe threw up her hands in frustrated disbelief. "You're impossible. Dr. Johnson said I should rest. He did not mean that I'm not allowed to stand up at all."

"That's not what I heard."

"Then you need to have your hearing checked."

"Maybe. But until the doctor says differently, bed rest means exactly that."

CeCe glared at him. "I'll call him tomorrow," she said with deadly calm.

"Fine. In the meantime…" He glanced around the room. "Do you sleep naked, or do you need a nightgown?"

CeCe felt her cheeks heat. She knew by the half smile that lifted the corner of his mouth that he was enjoying himself. "Naked," she said through her teeth, and was rewarded by the quick flare of fire in his eyes. "But tonight I'll wear a gown."

"Fine." *She said that on purpose,* he thought with admiration. "Where is it?"

"The dresser—second drawer," she said brusquely.

Zach pulled open the drawer and sifted through silky, colorful lingerie. He held up a lacy black teddy by its straps, half turning to lift an eyebrow inquiringly at CeCe. She flushed pinker, her eyes snapping.

"That's not it," she said tightly. "I want the blue flannel nightgown."

"That's a shame," Zach commented, returning the black lace to the drawer with obvious reluctance. He pulled out a flannel gown and shook out its voluminous folds, holding it out in front of him to observe it before shaking his head at CeCe. "Sorry, honey, but this can't hold a candle to the black one."

"Just give it to me," CeCe snapped. "And leave the room."

"Yes, ma'am."

Zach dropped the nightgown on her lap. She was steaming, her gray eyes shooting daggers at him and he couldn't resist bending closer. "I'd sure like to see you in the black one," he whispered, his voice husky and seductive.

Stunned, CeCe stared up at him. For a long moment, his heated gaze held hers, then his lashes lowered, veiling the hot need that smoldered in his eyes. He straightened and turned away from her to walk to the door. He stopped and half turned to look at her.

"I'll be back to tuck you in."

She was still speechless when he closed the door. She dragged in a deep breath, squeezed her eyes shut and mentally counted to ten, willing her pulse rate to slow down.

"Two weeks. I have two weeks to get through. Maybe I should have stayed in the hospital, even though it would have driven me crazy."

It was too late. She was here, in her own home, and Zach was going to be a constant distraction for at least two weeks. *Thank goodness he's determined that there won't be anything between us beyond a reluctant partnership due to Kenneth Hall's will,* she reminded herself. *Because I can't afford to trust the man. He has too many good reasons to wish me and my baby ill. And I'm not convinced I could tell him no if he really decided to turn up the heat.* Just remembering the banked fire that blazed from his blue eyes made her nerves shiver. She glanced at the closed door where he'd disappeared.

"He's probably standing outside in the hall, waiting for me to change into my nightclothes." She slipped off the bed and padded across the floor, turning the old-fashioned lock with a decisive click. She quickly stripped off her jeans and peeled her sweater off over her head, unhooking her bra to drop it atop the small pile of clothing.

She caught up her nightgown and poked her head through the unbuttoned bodice opening, quickly shoving her arms through the sleeves, and twitched the yards of flannel into place before turning sideways to the mirror. She smoothed the voluminous gown over the mound that was her growing stomach and patted the curve with affection.

The doorknob rattled and CeCe jumped, startled.

"CeCe?" Zach knocked, two sharp, demanding raps on the wooden panel. "Why is the door locked?"

"Because I wanted privacy." Irritated, she snatched up her jeans, sweater and bra, and hastily folded them across the dressing table's bench before she stomped to the door, unlocked it and threw it open.

Zach stood in the doorway, one hand braced against the doorjamb. His gaze scanned her quickly, head to toe, and his frown turned into an amused grin.

"What's so funny?" she demanded, hands on hips.

"I like the socks," he commented.

CeCe glanced down, lifting the hem of her nightgown. The wool socks that had kept her warm all day still covered her feet. She sniffed, turned on her heel and stalked to the bed to throw back the covers.

"I like them, too," she retorted. "They keep my feet warm."

She climbed into bed and sat propped against the headboard, tugging the sheet and blankets up to her waist. Angus shot past Zach and leaped up onto the bed, settling against her feet. CeCe folded her hands primly atop the blankets. "If you would be so kind as to turn off the overhead light," she said sweetly, "I'll go to sleep."

Zach stepped into the room, his palm brushing downward over the switch. The bright glare of the ceiling fixture was extinguished, leaving only the warm glow of the lamp on the bedside table. He crossed the room silently and tugged the blanket out of her fingers.

"Lie down."

The husky order was more invitation than command. CeCe fleetingly considered refusing him, to assert her independence, but the heat that lay deep in his eyes carried an unmistakable warning. Instead, she tugged her pillow out from behind her, plumping it with unnecessary force, before she slid beneath the covers and lay flat.

Zach eased the blanket higher and leaned over her, bracing a hand against the mattress on either side of her shoulders. "When I was a little boy and my mother tucked me in bed," he said, his voice slow and deep, "she always kissed me good-night."

"You're not my mother," CeCe said firmly. "And I'm not a little boy."

"That's true." He tucked the blankets around her shoulders before he turned off the lamp, throwing the room into shadowy darkness. Faint light spilled through the open door from the hallway and kept the room from being inky black.

CeCe's gaze followed the darker shadow that was Zach to the doorway, where he paused.

"Do you want the door left open?"

"Yes, please. If it's open and Angus wants to get up to roam about in the night, he won't wake me. If the door is closed, he'll walk up and down and pat my face with his paw until I get up and let him out."

"If he bothers you tonight, call me. I'll take care of him. You're not supposed to get out of bed."

"I know."

"Good night."

His voice was a soft, husky murmur in the darkness, filled with unspoken promise. CeCe drew a shaky breath. "Good night." Her own voice was unsteady.

She lay quietly, tracking his movements by the creak of the stairs as he climbed them, then the soft thud of his footfalls as he entered the upstairs bedroom directly above her. Moments later, she heard the faint creak of bedsprings, then silence fell.

Even though the sexual tension between them kept her on edge, there was something infinitely comforting about having Zach upstairs, within calling distance if she needed him. Much as she'd wanted to leave the hospital for the comfort of her own home, still she'd worried about being alone in the house if the cramps and bleeding recurred.

She realized with a start that Zach had distracted her so completely that she hadn't fretted over the safety of Baby all evening. *Did he purposely keep me busy?* she wondered. She curled on her side, one hand tucked beneath her pillow and cheek while she mulled over the possibility that Zach had spent the evening with her solely to divert her from worry over the baby. She still was uncertain of his motives, but there was no longer any doubt in her mind that he took his responsibilities as trustee of her child very seriously. Why else would he give up two weeks of his life to baby-sit her?

She yawned sleepily, gave Angus one last goodnight pat and closed her eyes.

CeCe's days and evenings settled into a comfortable routine. To her surprise, Zach stayed close to the house during the day, working in the machine shop and making frequent trips inside to check on her.

She wanted him. And although she told herself repeatedly that her hormones were running wild due to her pregnancy, the wanting didn't ease. She hung on to sanity with a thread, lectured herself daily, and counted the hours of each day, praying fervently that she'd make it through the two weeks without giving in and throwing herself at him.

After two weeks passed, Zach drove her to Butte Creek for her medical checkup. They both heaved a sigh of relief when Dr. Johnson told them that she was allowed to resume minimal activity interspersed with lots of rest. However, he didn't want her living alone. To their stunned surprise, Dr. Johnson told Zach that he needed to stay with CeCe for another week.

CeCe was ecstatic that the doctor was so pleased with her progress, but she wasn't at all sure how she was going to get through another week of sexual frustration.

"I'm sorry, Zach," she told him as they shed their coats in the hallway. "This is such an imposition. Why don't I call my mother and see if she can fly in to stay with me so you can get your life back to normal."

"No." Zach shook his head. "It's only another week. That's not long." He nearly groaned, thinking of the nightly cold showers awaiting him.

"If you're sure," CeCe said dubiously, eyeing the tense set of his shoulders and the hard line of his jaw. "I have to admit, I've grown accustomed to being treated like a princess, having you deliver tea to me and grant my every wish. You make a great personal slave, Zach.''

The taut lines of his face and body eased, and amusement lit his blue eyes. ''I'm beginning to think I've created a monster,'' he commented dryly.

''Oh, no,'' she said emphatically. ''Never. On the other hand...'' She eyed him consideringly. ''We need to talk about your tendency to believe that you're a general and I'm the army.''

''I *am* the general,'' he drawled lazily, enjoying the instant sparkle and snap that lit her eyes.

''I don't think so.'' She turned and led the way into the living room. ''What makes you think an army of one needs a general, anyway?''

''All armies need a general,'' he answered absently, his attention focused on the sway of her hips beneath the loose red wool jumper she wore over black tights. ''Regardless of how big or small they are.''

''Hmmph.'' CeCe sniffed in disbelief. ''I think the truth is that you're compulsive about giving orders.''

''I am not compulsive,'' he said with mild heat.

''That's debatable.'' CeCe seated herself in front of her loom and sighed with pleasure, abandoning the argument. She stroked her hand over the half-finished blanket in progress, the gesture eloquently loving. ''I've missed working,'' she said quietly.

Zach leaned against the wall, his hands tucked into his pockets, and watched her run her fingers in tactile delight over the bright blues and reds threaded onto the wooden loom.

"This means a lot to you, doesn't it?" he asked quietly, his gaze resting on her soft, contented smile.

"Yes." She nodded, glancing sideways at him. "I want to pass on to my own daughter all the things my grandmother taught me. I have wonderful memories of sitting on her lap while she worked and listening to the stories she told me about each piece she wove."

"You have the same look on your face that you get when you're talking about the baby," he commented.

"Really?" She smiled. "I suppose that's not surprising, since weaving and Baby are the two great loves in my life."

I want to be the third. The flash of instant reaction startled Zach.

"What is it?" CeCe wasn't sure what caused Zach's silent, intense scrutiny. He stared at her as if he'd never seen her before. Or as if she'd suddenly grown horns. She glanced downward, but found nothing amiss, then smoothed a hand self-consciously over her hair. "You're looking at me very strangely, Zach. Have I got a button unbuttoned, or grease on my face or something?"

"No." He strode toward the doorway leading to the hall, pausing on the threshold to look back at her. "I have to finish some work in the shop—shouldn't be more than an hour or two. Don't start dinner. I'll do it when I come in."

And he was gone.

CeCe heard the small sounds he made as he retrieved his coat and hat, followed by the opening and closing of the front door.

She sat motionless for several moments, staring in confusion at the empty doorway, listening to the silence he left behind in the house.

"What was that all about?" she murmured.

Angus prowled down the hallway and across the living room to her side, twining around her ankles and purring loudly in a blatant demand for attention. CeCe leaned awkwardly forward and picked him up, cradling him on her knee while she stroked his fur.

"I wish you could talk, Angus. I need an explanation of the male psyche."

Angus bumped his head against her chin in response and CeCe laughed, hugging him before she settled him back on the floor.

"No comment? In that case, you can be my furry foot-warmer while I work."

She put aside Zach's puzzling expression and began to weave, quickly losing herself in the rhythmic motions.

CeCe thought Zach was quieter than usual that evening, but accepted his explanation that he was preoccupied with work. The next morning, he drove off shortly after breakfast; she was at her loom just before lunch when she heard him return. She glanced out the window and across the stretch of snowy yard to the barn where Zach's truck was backed up to the wide doors, the bed of the pickup half-loaded with bales of hay.

He shoved the wide doors open and backed the truck inside the barn, then slid the doors closed once more, shutting him away from CeCe's sight.

I wonder what he's doing? she thought, her curiosity aroused. She waited impatiently for him to appear for lunch and was nearly ready to don coat and hat to trudge through the snow to the barn, when the wide doors slid open and the pickup emerged. He parked the truck and stepped out to close the barn doors before he climbed back into the cab and drove to the house.

CeCe left the loom and hurried to the entryway, flinging open the door. Her breath caught at the frosty air and she wrapped her arms around her middle in an effort to fend off the cold while she waited for Zach to turn off the engine and reach the sidewalk.

"What are you doing?" she called.

The snow glittered like diamonds under the winter sun. She shielded her eyes with her hand as Zach walked up the sidewalk toward her.

"Don't stand out here in the cold," he scolded, taking the steps in two long strides. Catching her elbow, he urged her ahead of him into the house, pushing the door nearly closed behind them.

"Why did you put hay in the barn?" she asked, watching him take her coat off the hook.

"Because there wasn't any there. Here, put your hand in the sleeve."

CeCe cooperated, shoving her arms through the sleeves. "You didn't answer my question." He wrapped her muffler around her throat once, twice, the second time high enough to cover her mouth. "Mmmph." Her eyes shot daggers at him. She swatted his hand away and tugged the wool scarf below her chin. "Yuck. Now I have fuzzies on my tongue."

He shook his head. "Fuzzies?"

"Yes, you know." She waved her hand in a vague gesture. "The little filament things wool sheds."

He grinned at her. "For a woman who's crazy about wool, you're awfully vague about technical words."

She planted her hands on her hips and glared at him. "I don't have to be technical—I'm an artist." She suddenly realized that while she'd been distracted by his antics, he'd managed to bundle her up and outside to the yard gate where she planted her feet and stopped.

He tugged on her arm. She firmly removed it from his grasp and refused to move.

"What are you doing?" he asked.

"Ah. Precisely the question I want answered," she told him with deadly politeness. "In fact, I believe those were my exact words not five minutes ago. You have yet to answer them."

"I was hoping you hadn't noticed," he said wryly.

"I noticed."

"I don't suppose you'd consider waiting for an answer until we're inside the barn, where it's warm?"

She considered for a moment. "All right." He cupped her elbow in his hand and urged her forward. "But only because if we go into the barn, I can see for myself what you were doing, since it's becoming blindingly clear that you're not going to tell me."

"I'll tell you—when we get there." This time it was Zach who stopped. He looked down at her in consternation. "Damn. I forgot you're only supposed to have moderate exercise. Come here."

With practised ease, he picked her up and strode toward the barn.

"Zach," CeCe protested. "You've got to get over this habit of carrying me around like a child."

Zach's swift glance was searing. "Believe me, honey," he said bluntly, "I've never once thought of you as a child. And I never will."

Chapter Ten

CeCe didn't have a response. She wasn't sure what a woman was supposed to say to a man when he looked at her as if he were starving and he'd like to have her for dinner.

Zach set her on her feet and opened the barn door, hustling her inside and sliding it closed behind them.

CeCe looked around with interest, her gaze darting down the wide aisle that bisected the long section and the stalls on either side. A stack of hay bales sat against the outside wall of a stall nearly halfway down the aisle. She sniffed appreciatively. "I can smell the hay," she commented. "Is that all you did today— move hay into the barn?"

"Not exactly."

CeCe glanced sideways at him. He was being very

evasive. "What *exactly* did you do?" she asked curiously.

"It's easier to show you than to explain." Zach cupped her elbow in his palm, shortening his long strides to match her shorter steps as they moved down the aisle. He stopped at the near edge of the stack of hay bales. "This is it."

CeCe glanced at the hay in confusion. "The hay?"

"No." He shook his head and nudged her forward. "Sorry, I forgot that you couldn't see over the bales." He halted abruptly just past the hay and nodded at the stall.

"Oh, Zach!" CeCe gasped in disbelief. Fresh straw was strewn ankle deep in the stall, and lying in the center, contentedly chewing their cud, were Matilda and another of Duncan Burke's prize ewes. Their ears swiveled and they lurched to their feet at CeCe's voice, swiftly approaching the gate to poke their noses between the wide boards. CeCe reached through the gate and rubbed their heads, delighted when they responded by butting against her palm in a bid for more attention.

"What are they doing here?" CeCe looked over her shoulder at Zach. He stood watching her with a half smile on his face, leaning against the stack of baled hay.

"They live here," he said.

She straightened, giving the ewes one last affectionate pat. "Zachariah Colby, if you make me pry information out of you about these sheep, I swear I'm going to smack you."

Zach grinned and held up a hand in surrender.

"Duncan says their names are Matilda and Carmen. He said to tell you that he would never have sold them to me if he didn't know that you would take care of them as well as he would."

"You bought them? For me?"

Happiness bubbled like champagne through her veins. CeCe took two running steps and threw herself at him, looping her arms around his neck with an exuberance that knocked his hat off and sent them both reeling backward. Had it not been for the solid stack of hay at Zach's back, they would have hit the floor.

Zach wrapped his arms around her, holding her safe and laughing at the childlike delight that lit her face. She went up on her toes to reach him, tugging his head down to kiss him. A simple kiss that quickly turned serious.

CeCe wasn't sure how it happened, but a kiss to say thank you suddenly had her swamped in desire, lust and need. She moaned softly, pressing closer, her skin heating feverishly as his lips moved with hot demand against hers. Zach's arms tightened and she tried desperately to get closer, frustrated with the jackets and clothing that kept her skin from his.

The sharp bleat of sheep startled them. Zach's hands tightened on her body, his head lifting swiftly before CeCe felt the tension ease from the hard body she lay against. Slowly, she dropped back onto her heels, leaning against him for support.

"Thank you for buying Matilda and Carmen," she said, her voice unsteady. His eyes smoldered with dark blue fire, his hair mussed where she'd threaded her fingers through it.

"Do you always kiss men who buy you gifts?" he asked.

She thought about his question for a moment. "I'm not sure," she confessed. "No one has ever bought me a gift quite like this one before."

"Honey, if two ewes earn me a kiss like that one, I'd love to see what I'd get if I bought you a whole herd of Duncan's sheep."

CeCe felt her cheeks flush hotter. "Try it," she dared him, her voice husky with the storm of emotion that still hummed in her veins.

He shook his head slowly, amusement slowly tamping down the hard edge of arousal that burned in his eyes. He shifted, holding her steady while she eased away from him, and then stood upright himself. He collected his hat and settled it on his head, tugging it down over his forehead, before he looked at the sheep.

"If anyone had told me that I'd ever buy sheep, I'd have punched them in the nose and called them a liar," he said with self-derision. He looked at CeCe and shook his head. "Women. You're all a great deal of trouble."

CeCe didn't take offense. Instead, she laughed and tucked her hand into the crook of his elbow, eyeing the two female sheep fondly. "But we're worth it, aren't we, girls?" She glanced up at Zach. "What made you change your mind? Whenever I mentioned sheep before today, you nearly bit my head off. You were adamant about never owning sheep."

"I don't own them," Zach denied swiftly. "You do. And you changed my mind when you were talking about your love of weaving and passing on your grandmother's stories to your daughter. Everyone should get to see at least one of their dreams come true." He looked down at her, his deep voice softly solemn, rich with conviction. "I want that for you."

CeCe swallowed, the lump in her throat boulder-size. She couldn't speak, and tears threatened, so she brushed a soft kiss against his cheek.

"Thank you," she whispered.

"You're welcome," he murmured in reply, well pleased with her pleasure in his gift.

"Ouch. Oooh."

The muted groans woke him in the middle of the night. His eyes flicked open and for one startled moment he stared at the dark ceiling, wondering if he was imagining the sounds. Below him, CeCe moaned again. He threw back the covers and sat up, grabbing his jeans and dragging them on. He raced down the stairs, managing to shove the bottom three buttons through their holes before he reached CeCe's bedroom door.

"CeCe?" The only response he got was a groan of pain. Zach fumbled his way across the dark bedroom to the bedside table and switched on the lamp. CeCe was sitting up in bed, covers thrown back, her nightgown bunched above her knees, clutching her left calf.

"Damn. Damn. Damn." She chanted the swearword under her breath, grimacing with pain.

"CeCe, what's the matter? Are you hurt—is it the baby?"

"No." She rubbed her calf harder. "I have a charley horse in my leg and it won't go away."

"Geez." Zach slumped with relief. He dropped onto the foot of the bed facing her and pushed her hands out of the way. "Here, let me do that."

The muscle was cramped in a tight knot. Zach's firm grip and the sure strokes of his powerful fingers were just short of pain, but the cramp eased and CeCe sighed with relief. She threaded her fingers through the tangle of her hair and pushed the heavy mane back over her shoulder.

Zach continued to knead her calf, smoothing away the remains of the muscle cramp. The yellow lamplight gleamed off his bare shoulders; his blond hair was tousled by sleep and he'd clearly leaped out of bed and yanked on his jeans before he raced downstairs. His broad chest was bare, the smooth, hard muscles roughened by a vee of gold hair that narrowed across the washboard muscles of his midriff. The gold became a narrow line below his navel and disappeared inside the partially buttoned waistband of his jeans. Her heart lurched and picked up speed. Now that the pain in her leg was nearly gone, her body was obviously ready to focus on other, more appealing, needs.

She sighed aloud and Zach glanced up.

"Better?" he asked.

"Yes, much."

His gaze held hers, his fingers easing their strong massage until their movements became slow, testing circles against her skin. He watched her eyes turn lambent, the gray growing darker, smokier. The steady burn of fire in his veins climbed ever higher with each stroke of his hands against her leg and he knew she felt the same heat. He smoothed his palm upward and stroked his thumb in rhythmic fascination over the tender, sensitive skin on the back of her knee.

"I don't know how long I can sleep under the same roof with you and stay out of your bed," he said bluntly, his voice deeper, raspy with the effort it took to speak. "Ask me in."

"Zach." CeCe spread her hands and glanced downward, where the flannel gown draped over the undeniable swell of her belly. "I'm pregnant."

He sighed heavily. "I know."

"In case you haven't noticed, that makes me fat and about as lacking in sex appeal as a brown paper bag."

He stared at her in disbelief. "Where the hell did you get that idea?"

"From my mirror."

"Your mirror lied."

CeCe eyed him helplessly, completely disconcerted. "Zach."

His heart turned over with an ache at the yearning contained in that one word. "Let me hold you. I'm going crazy trying to keep myself from touching you. I know we can't actually make love," he told her. "It wouldn't be safe for the baby."

"Actually," CeCe whispered, distracted. "Dr. Johnson told me that it was perfectly safe."

"He told you that it's safe for you to make love?" he demanded.

"Well, yes."

Zach's blue eyes turned nearly black. CeCe shivered. His thumb left the back of her knee and his hand smoothed up her thigh.

CeCe drew in a shaky breath. "Zach, I think we should talk about this, don't you?"

His fingertips found the soft skin of her inner thigh and lingered, the seductive, sure strokes sending her blood pressure skyrocketing.

"Only if you're considering saying no," he told her.

She stared into his eyes, mesmerized by the hot lights that danced in the blue depths.

"You know this is probably not a good idea," she felt compelled to say, her lashes half closing in response to the surges of heat that pulsed in her veins with each stroke of his fingers.

His gaze didn't leave hers, but recognition of her concession leaped in his eyes. In one smooth movement, he was beside her, his hand on her thigh smoothing her nightgown higher while his mouth unerringly found hers.

CeCe fell backward on the bed, her hands closing over his shoulders. Zach's mouth left hers to trail hotly down the curve of her throat and she tilted her head back against the pillow to give him access, nearly purring with pleasure. His lips reached the barrier of her nightgown and he growled in frustration, his hand leaving her thigh to slip buttons free on the gown's bodice. CeCe felt her nightgown loosen and her eyes flew open. Her fingers caught his and his gaze lifted to meet hers.

"The lamp," she said throatily.

"You want it off?" he asked.

"Please."

The anxiety and self-consciousness in her eyes stopped any argument he would have made. He cupped her cheek and smoothed his thumb over the lush, faintly swollen curve of her lower lip. The soft dampness of her mouth was an irresistible lure and he bent closer, tracing with his tongue the path his thumb had made. He lingered, unwilling and unable to cease, until he reluctantly forced himself to lift away from her. He stretched across her and snapped off the lamp, throwing the room into darkness.

"Thank you." Her voice was a soft, heated murmur in the darkness.

"Just so you know," he said, stroking his fingers through the silk of her hair. "I only turned off the lamp because you wanted me to. I think you're beautiful."

He smoothed his fingertips across her mouth and felt the smile that curved her lips. He kissed the corner of her smile and returned to freeing the buttons that marched halfway down her gown. Drunk on the feel of satiny skin beneath his hands, he brushed his mouth down her throat, loving the way she arched to meet him, and pushed aside the open gown. Her skin was hot, satiny smooth against his cheek when he brushed the inner curve of her breast, and she jerked in response, her fingers tightening over his shoulders before they loosened and smoothed over his biceps, subtly urging him closer.

The darkness precluded CeCe's ability to see Zach, but intensified all her other senses. Her body felt alive with millions of sensitive nerve endings, all of them reacting to the smooth, sure stroke of Zach's warm hands and the warm, damp movements of his mouth against her skin. He shifted her, turning her on her side to face him, and slipped his leg between hers. The heavy muscles of his thigh nudged her, and deep in her body, need coiled tighter until she thought she'd scream.

"Zach, please," she groaned. But then his mouth closed over the crest of her breast and she forgot everything else.

Zach felt her quickened breathing and slipped a hand between her thighs. Seconds later, she cried out with release and buried her face against the curve of his shoulder while aftershocks slowly ebbed. He continued to stroke his hand over soft curves and silky skin, content for the moment to hold her while he waited for her to recover.

CeCe wasn't sure just when the slow pleasure of his hand exploring the slope of her breast and smoothing over her thigh ceased being comforting and became arousing once more. She only knew that her body responded with growing eagerness. She pressed a kiss to the sleek skin of his shoulder before tilting her head back, skimming her lips along his neck and the underside of his jaw. He caught his breath in an indrawn hiss before he took her mouth with his in an openmouthed, wet kiss that set fire to the smoldering heat that once more moved through her veins.

Her hands left his back and smoothed down his sides, stroking over the muscles of his midriff. But when she was frustrated by the barrier of his jeans and tugged impatiently at the waistband, Zach groaned and covered her hand with his, holding her fingers still against his bare skin.

She eased her lips a breath away from his.

"Zach? What's wrong?"

"Nothing, honey, nothing at all," he said raspily, struggling for control.

"Then why did you stop me?"

"Because if you touch me, I won't be able to stop."

Bewildered, CeCe strained to see his face in the darkened room. "You want to stop?" Her voice reflected her confusion and an underlying tremor of hurt.

"No," he said gruffly. "But I have to—I won't chance hurting you or the baby."

"Zach, you won't hurt us," she murmured reassuringly. "I was worried about the baby and asked Dr. Johnson in detail about what I could and couldn't do. He ran through a whole, long list of activities that wouldn't harm me or Baby—including making love."

"Damn, I want to believe that," he said tightly, his hand moving compulsively over the satiny skin on the inside of her thigh, his fingertips brushing the silky damp thatch. Her hips lifted involuntarily in response and he groaned again. "Help me, CeCe. Tell me no."

"But I don't want to," she whispered, her lips

brushing against his as she spoke. She eased her fingers inside the half-fastened opening of his jeans and found him. He swore softly, his body tensing until her hand fisted around him and his hips jerked in reaction. "Please," she murmured.

He wasn't superhuman. He would have had to have been to deny her. He ripped open the remaining buttons on his jeans and endured the sweet torture of her hand on him as long as he could.

"Enough." He barely managed to get the word out, slipping her hand from him as he gently turned her until her back was to him, the sweet curve of her hips cradled against his. He clenched his teeth against the almost painful pleasure as he slowly entered her until he was seated, solid and deep. Nearly mindless with pleasure, he held on to sanity with only a thread. "All right?" he asked, his voice a deepened, hoarse growl of sound.

"Yes," she gasped in response, pushing back against him while her nails scored half moons in his arm just below her breasts.

Zach lost any hope of control. Her soft moans pushed him over the edge and he gave in to the need that drove him to completion. Vaguely, he knew that CeCe exploded with him, but it wasn't until it was over and they lay, curled spoonlike and exhausted, that he realized he'd lost the ability to guarantee gentleness.

He propped himself up on one elbow and shifted her onto her back so he could see her, but the darkness in the room frustrated him. He twisted and flicked on the lamp behind him, turning back to find her watching him through half-closed eyes, a contented smile curving the lush line of her lips.

Relief washed over him.

"I hope that smile means you're all right," he said, smoothing the silky tangle of her hair from her cheek.

"I'm better than all right," she assured him. She laid her open palm on his chest, just over his still-racing heart. "How about you?"

"I'm fine. The important question is, did I hurt you?"

Her eyes widened. "No." His blue eyes were dark with worry and self-recrimination as they searched hers. "Zach, stop worrying," she said softly, gently rubbing away the frown lines from between his eyebrows before her fingertip traced the line of his scar down his cheek to his mouth. "Not only did you not hurt me, you made me feel wonderful, the best I've felt in years."

The tight band of guilt encircling his chest eased. Zach caught her fingers and pressed a kiss into her palm. "You wouldn't lie to me, would you?"

"Never."

"Good. Because you made me feel pretty great, too."

"Yeah?" She smiled, a cat-who-ate-the-canary sort of smile. She felt well loved and well pleasured and not at all like a staid, about-to-be mother. "You're not one of those men who has a thing for pregnant women, are you?"

He grinned lazily, amusement lighting his eyes and chasing away the last traces of worry. "Not unless the pregnant woman happens to be named Cecelia."

"Good." CeCe stretched lazily and wrapped her arms around his neck, tugging him down until his lips nearly touched hers. "In that case, do you suppose we could try that again?"

Zach had lived with his ex-wife for a short six months, but it hadn't prepared him for living with CeCe. Making love with the pregnant widow was like nothing he'd ever experienced before. She was sensual, earthy and always eager—everything he'd ever wanted in a woman in his hottest dreams.

He refused, however, to consider the possibility that what he felt for CeCe was love. He couldn't deny that he was overwhelmingly attracted to her physically. In addition, he was becoming increasingly possessive and felt a strong sense of responsibility for her and her unborn child, and the sheer contentment he knew when she was with him was undeniable.

Why living with her was so satisfying, he didn't know. God knew she wasn't an easygoing, biddable woman—in fact, she was just the opposite. She argued heatedly with him about any number of subjects and adamantly refused to allow him to treat her like an invalid.

He decided that he'd finally met a woman that he could marry for purely practical, logical reasons. And one that he wouldn't have to lay his heart on the line by saying *I love you* to.

So, one afternoon in the practical light of day, he proposed.

"I think we should get married."

CeCe almost choked on a mouthful of herbal tea.

"I'm sorry." She coughed, clearing her throat before she could say any more. "What did you say?"

"I said, I think we should get married."

"Oh." Curled into the corner of the sofa, an afghan spread across her lap with Angus purring sleepily beside her, CeCe lowered her hot teacup carefully to the sofa arm and eyed him. "Why?"

"Why?" That wasn't exactly the response Zach had been hoping for. He shifted against the cushions at the other end of the sofa and focused on the tips of his stocking feet stretched out in front of him. "There are a lot of good reasons," he said finally. "We get along pretty well. If we lived together permanently, you wouldn't be alone here by yourself with the baby. And the baby—she would be better if there was a man here, for a father figure, you know?" He ground to a halt, frowning intently at the tips of his toes, before he darted a sideways glance at her. She was watching him with an interested expression. "The neighbors are going to talk if we're not married and I stay here much longer, and I'll be damned if I'll leave you alone while you're pregnant. And we're great in bed together," he finished, flashing her a slow smile.

She laughed, returning his steamy smile with a slanted glance that raised his blood pressure.

"There is that," she agreed. "Is that all of the reasons?"

"Isn't that enough? People have gotten married for a lot less."

"Mmm," she murmured noncommittally. *He*

didn't say he loves me. Disappointment dulled the bright flash of delight.

"I'm not sure that we should get married for those reasons, Zach. I'm perfectly willing to let you be involved in Baby's life, in fact, I plan to encourage you, but I don't believe that two people should get married for convenience. I think marriage is difficult at best, and comfort and convenience simply aren't a strong enough foundation to build a lifelong marriage on. If we were in love, that would be different, but as it is, once the baby is born, I think you should move out."

He stiffened, his eyes narrowing, the muscles flexing in his jaw.

"So you're willing to sleep with me for a while, but I'm not good enough to have around permanently?"

"No, that's not what I meant at all." CeCe reached for him, closing her fingers over the tense muscles of his forearm. "If it were only me, I'd stay just as we are, but I'll be responsible for another life when the baby arrives. I know it may sound old-fashioned, but I won't live with a man I'm not married to because I want to teach my child to respect traditional morals."

Zach searched her face. Her golden eyes reflected the same depth of yearning and mixed emotions that were in his own heart, her grip on his forearm tight with strain. The visible proof that she was clearly as torn and confused as he was calmed him, and he sighed. Emotional stress wasn't good for CeCe and the baby.

"All right." He picked up Angus and set him, protesting mildly, on the floor. Then he gathered up

CeCe, afghan and all, and settled her on his lap. He refused to think about his driving need to put a ring on her finger and legally claim her, and instead, focused on her willingness to admit that she craved the hot kisses and earthshaking lovemaking they shared every bit as much as he did. "We'll talk about this again after the baby is born."

CeCe's baby decided to arrive two weeks early.

"Zach. Zach?" CeCe shook him.

"Mmph." He woke, rolling over in bed to squint up at her. "What is it, honey?"

"I think we need to go to the hospital."

Zach sat bolt upright, the covers falling to his waist. "The baby? Are you sure?"

"Yes, I'm sure."

He threw back the covers and reached for his jeans, yanking them on as he stood. "I'll call Dr. Johnson and start the truck. Can you get dressed?"

"Of course," she said calmly, sliding from the far side of the bed.

Fifteen minutes later, Zach was peering through the windshield and swearing under his breath at the late spring snow that piled against the wiper blades.

"What rotten luck," he growled, shooting a quick glance at CeCe. "Don't worry, honey, this snowstorm may slow us down a little, but we'll get there in time."

CeCe managed a smile. "Good, I would really rather not give birth in your truck cab," she joked, only half teasing.

"Geez, no," he said fervently. "Can't you hold your breath or something?"

CeCe laughed, breaking off in midchuckle to clutch her middle with both hands. "I don't think holding my breath would stop labor," she said when she could speak again.

"Then pray," he said shortly, softening the command with a quick grin. "And let's hope God didn't plan to have me deliver this kid."

The wet snowflakes were still coming down in a thick, silent fall when Zach braked in front of the emergency room. His boots slipped in the inches of wetness that covered the slick tarmac as he rounded the cab and pulled open the passenger door.

"I'm going to carry you, CeCe. The snow is half slush, and the pavement's as slippery as ice." He leaned in and picked her up just as another labor pain gripped her belly and she groaned, panting shallowly in an effort to ride the pain. Her hands gripped the front of his jacket, closing into fists. "Hold on, sweetheart." He slammed the pickup door and bent his head to shield her from the wet snow as he carefully made his way across the few feet of slick pavement to the entrance.

The nurse on duty behind the reception desk rose immediately when he swept through the automatic doors and strode swiftly toward her.

"Hello, Dr. Johnson called and said you were on your way." She bustled ahead of Zach and pushed the button for the elevator. "We'll take her straight upstairs to obstetrics. If you'll wait a moment, I'll get a wheelchair."

"No." Zach stepped into the waiting elevator. "I'll carry her."

The nurse hurriedly followed them into the elevator and punched the button for the second floor. Zach carried CeCe off the elevator and down the hall to the room the nurse directed him to, but then the nurses there shooed him outside and told him to go to the waiting room. He went reluctantly, shedding his coat and hat before he began pacing the length of the room.

"Mr. Colby?"

Zach spun swiftly. A young nurse stood just inside the door at the far end of the room.

"Yes?"

"Ms. Hawkins is settled in her room and would like you to join her."

"Thanks." Zach followed the nurse from the room, but quickly outpaced her, his long strides eating up the distance down the hall to the room where he'd left CeCe. He paused in the doorway, unnoticed. She wore a white hospital gown and was tucked into a bed with lowered rails.

"Hi," he called softly. She turned her head on the pillow and smiled a welcome. Relieved, he crossed the room and sank onto the armchair next to the bed. "Has the doctor been in to see you?"

"Yes. He says everything is going well." Her eyes twinkled. "Were you really afraid that you would have to deliver Baby in your truck?"

"I had a few bad moments during the drive here," he admitted. "Is this baby arriving early, or did you miscalculate your due date?"

"Baby is arriving a little early," she conceded. "I'll have to have a talk with her when she gets here. Her mother likes to make plans and follow schedules, and she upset both. And I considered natural childbirth and rejected it in favor of the hospital setting. Your truck cab wasn't even a possibility when I made plans for this delivery."

"Hmm." Zach grinned. "Just as long as she gets here, safe and sound, I won't say a word."

"Did you call Sarah and Jennifer?"

"Not yet," Zach answered. "To tell you the truth, I was too worried about you to remember to call, but there's a telephone at the end of the hall. I'll phone them in a few minutes."

"Will you ask Sarah to cancel my hair appointment?"

Zach stared at her, bemused. "How can you remember a hair appointment at a time like this?"

"I don't know," she admitted. "I keep wondering what else I've forgotten to do. I thought I had at least two more weeks to prepare for labor."

"You are amazing," Zach shook his head.

CeCe reached out and took his hand, but before she could speak, another labor pain began to build. "Uh-oh," she told him. "Here comes another one."

Dawn came and the morning hours wore on to noon. Zach stayed with CeCe, holding her hand, giving her ice water, wiping her forehead, and learning a new respect for the strength she owned in her small body as the labor built in intensity. It was late afternoon before Dr. Johnson finally announced that it was time to wheel CeCe to the delivery room.

Zach brushed one last kiss against her cheek, standing motionless in the hallway until the delivery-room doors closed behind the doctor, nurses and the gurney that held CeCe before he reluctantly returned to the crowded waiting room. One by one, he answered questions about CeCe's progress from Sarah, Jennifer and their husbands before he could retreat into silent worrying.

He hated the waiting. Hated the feeling of helplessness that kept him pacing from windows to door and back again.

Hands jammed into his jeans pockets, he stared unseeingly out the window at the snow-covered parking lot below.

What if something goes wrong?

The possibility that he could lose CeCe in that room didn't bear thinking about, but he couldn't shove the thought from his mind. Just as impossible to accept was that anything might happen to the baby they wanted so desperately. *They?*

His hands clenched into fists as the realization hit him that he wanted CeCe's baby with a depth of emotion that stunned him. When had he started thinking of CeCe's baby as theirs? Had it happened the first time he'd felt the little one move inside CeCe? Or had the feeling grown so slowly that he hadn't noticed the subtle changes?

"Zach? Zach?"

The male voice interrupted his thoughts and he

glanced over his shoulder. Dr. Johnson stood in the open doorway, grinning broadly.

"Is she all right?"

"She's fine—better than fine, actually." The doctor chuckled and crossed the room. "She's the mother of a beautiful little girl and both baby and mommy came through with flying colors."

Zach drew a deep breath and took the doctor's outstretched hand, shaking it numbly. "Good—that's good," he mumbled.

"Cecelia and her little girl are back in their room if you want to visit them," the doctor said kindly.

"Thanks, Doc." Zach's voice held heartfelt, sincere appreciation.

"Don't mention it, Zach." Dr. Johnson clapped him on the back just as a female voice paged him over the speaker system. He sighed and shook his head. "I have to go. Tell Cecelia I'll drop in to check on her and the baby before I leave the hospital tonight."

"Right—I will."

Zach shoved open the door to CeCe's room and stepped inside, pausing at the sight of CeCe and the pink-blanket-wrapped bundle tucked next to her on the bed.

She looked up and smiled and Zach's shaken world settled back on its axis. He crossed the room and bent to press a swift, fierce kiss on her mouth.

"You scared the hell out of me," he whispered against her lips.

CeCe gazed up at him, struck speechless by the

naked emotion in his eyes. Before she could reassure him, the baby stirred, muttering soft little noises.

Zach's gaze darted to the little girl. "What's wrong?"

"Nothing." CeCe smiled and cuddled the baby closer. "Jessica Rose just wants a little attention. Would you like to hold her?" she asked him.

"Do you think I should?" He eyed the tiny girl with trepidation.

"Of course." CeCe eased the baby out of her arms and Zach took her awkwardly. He handled the precious bundle as if she were made of glass, and the awestruck look in his eyes melted CeCe's heart. *If I didn't already love him,* she thought mistily, *I'd fall in love with him right now, this very moment.*

He carried the baby to the window and held her up, easing the blanket away so he could see her. "Look at you," he crooned softly, his voice deep with affection. "You've got your mama's hair, and her eyes. Lucky little girl, you're going to be as pretty as your mommy."

He glanced back at CeCe and found her watching him. Exhausted from her struggle to bring Jessica into the world, still the strength of the love that lit her smile wrapped him and the baby he held in a warmth that wiped away his own weariness and made him feel ten feet tall.

Why haven't I told her that I love her? The deep, solid certainty that he loved her was irrefutable. Why he'd waited so long to tell her suddenly made no sense to Zach, nor did any of the reasons he'd had for denying his need of her.

no. You also said that we'd talk about it later. I want you to marry me, CeCe.''

Stunned, CeCe stared at him. She'd braced herself to hear him tell her he was leaving; she was completely unprepared to hear a second marriage proposal.

"Zach, I don't—"

"Shh." Zach stopped her words with his forefinger laid gently against her lips.

"Before you refuse, I want you to know that I'm asking because I love you. I know I gave you a lot of practical reasons before, and those are still all true. But none of them mean anything compared to the fact that life without you wouldn't mean a thing." Beneath his finger, her mouth curved slowly upward in a tremulous smile, the dove gray eyes that gazed into his misty with unshed tears.

"I hope that smile means yes," he said, his voice husky with emotion. His hand left her mouth and tucked a strand of dark silky hair over her shoulder before dropping to rest on her thigh.

"You love me," she whispered. She traced the hard lines of his face—the high arch of his cheeks, the curve of his eyebrows, the stubborn angles of jaw and chin. His eyes drifted nearly closed, gleaming with blue fire through the thick shield of his lashes as he watched her intently. CeCe brushed her mouth against his. "I love you, too." His hands tightened on her waist and thigh to pull her closer, but she placed her open palm against his chest, stopping him. "But I'm worried about Jessica."

Confusion etched a faint frown between his eyebrows. "Jessica? What about Jessica?"

"Jessica's biological father is Aaron Hall—and you hated Aaron. Goodness knows you had good cause to despise him, but nevertheless, how will you be able to accept his daughter. My daughter."

Zach's thumb drew small, soothing circles on the denim covering her thigh. "I won't deny that there was no love lost between me and Aaron," he admitted. "But ever since I held Jessica in my arms, I've thought of her as mine. It wasn't Aaron who held you at night and felt her kick inside you, and it wasn't Aaron who held her right after she was born. I fell in love with her at first sight, just like I fell in love with you the night I saw you standing beside the road in a snowstorm. Although with Jessica, I admitted it right away. With you, it took a little longer, or maybe I fought it a little harder."

"You're pretty terrific, Zach," she said softly.

"So are you, CeCe," he replied, with a grin. His face sobered. "I don't want anyone saying I married you for Jessie's inheritance. I've given some thought to the problem and I'd like to put the entire Hall estate in trust for our Jessie and any other kids we may have. What do you think?"

"I think that's a wonderful idea." CeCe blinked away tears and wondered mistily if he realized how revealing it was that he thought of Jessica as "our Jessie."

"Good." He glanced around the room. "You've done wonders with this old house, but my place is bigger. I'd like you to look over the house, see if you think you could live there."

"Does it bother you? Living in the house your father built?" she asked with sympathy.

"Kenneth Hall didn't build this house."

"Are you sure?" she asked, puzzled. "I could have sworn that Aaron told me his father built this house for his mother for their twenty-fifth wedding anniversary."

"He built her a house, but it wasn't this one. The new house burned down after his parents died and Aaron moved back here. This house was built by Kenneth's grandfather sometime during the late 1930s or early 1940s."

"Oh. I see." CeCe glanced around the solid, old-fashioned square room. "I wonder what reason Aaron had for lying to me."

"Aaron never needed a reason to lie," Zach told her, his voice hardening. "But he might have thought you'd be more interested in his plan to give him an heir if the property had a newer, bigger house."

"If he'd known me better," CeCe remarked, "he would have known that an older, solid house was more of an enticement." She cupped his chin, gazing intently into his eyes. "A lot of what he told me about himself wasn't true, or a half truth at best, but it doesn't really matter, Zach. He's gone, and we're here, and so is Jessica. Regardless of whether he tricked us both or used me to produce a child only because of his father's will, the end result is wonderful. You love me, and Jessica and I love you."

A slow smile spread over Zach's face, easing the

tension from his jaw and forehead. "You're right," he murmured. His gaze searched hers, his smile growing. "You know," he added, his voice deeper, smokier. "We need to talk about making some more babies."

CeCe laughed, visions of children with Zach's blond hair and blue eyes dancing behind her closed eyelids as his mouth took hers.

* * * * *

Silhouette Books is delighted to alert you to a brand-new MacGregor story from Nora Roberts, coming in October 1998, from Silhouette Special Edition. Look for

THE WINNING HAND

and find out how a small-town librarian wins the heart of elusive, wealthy and darkly handsome Robert "Mac" Blade.

Here's a sneak preview of

THE WINNING HAND....

The Winning Hand

There was something wonderfully smooth under her cheek. Silk, satin, Darcy thought dimly. She'd always loved the feel of silk. Once she'd spent nearly her entire paycheck on a silk blouse, creamy white with gold, heart shaped buttons. She'd had to skip lunch for two weeks, but it had been worth it every time she slipped that silk over her skin.

She sighed, remembering it.

"Come on, all the way out."

"What?" She blinked her eyes open, focused on a slant of light from a jeweled lamp.

"Here, try this." Mac slipped a hand under her head, lifted it, and put a glass of water to her lips.

"What?"

"You're repeating yourself. Drink some water."

"Okay." She sipped obediently, studying the

tanned, long-fingered hand that held the glass. She was on a bed, she realized now, a huge bed with a silky cover. There was a mirrored ceiling over her head. "Oh my." Warily, she shifted her gaze until she saw his face.

He set the glass aside, then sat on the edge of the bed, noting with amusement that she scooted over slightly to keep more distance between them. "Mac Blade. I run this place."

"Darcy. I'm Darcy Wallace. Why am I here?"

"It seemed better than leaving you sprawled on the floor of the casino. You fainted."

"I did?" Mortified, she closed her eyes again. "Yes, I guess I did. I'm sorry."

"It's not an atypical reaction to winning close to two million dollars."

Her eyes popped open, her hand grabbed at her throat. "I'm sorry. I'm still a little confused. Did you say I won almost two million dollars?"

"You put the money in, you pulled the lever, you hit." There wasn't an ounce of color in her cheeks, he noted, and thought she looked like a bruised fairy. "Do you want to see a doctor?"

"No, I'm just…I'm okay. I can't think. My head's spinning."

"Take your time." Instinctively, he plumped up the pillows behind her and eased her back.

"I had nine dollars and thirty-seven cents when I got here."

"Well, now you have $1 800 088.37."

"Oh. Oh." Shattered, she put her hands over her face and burst into tears.